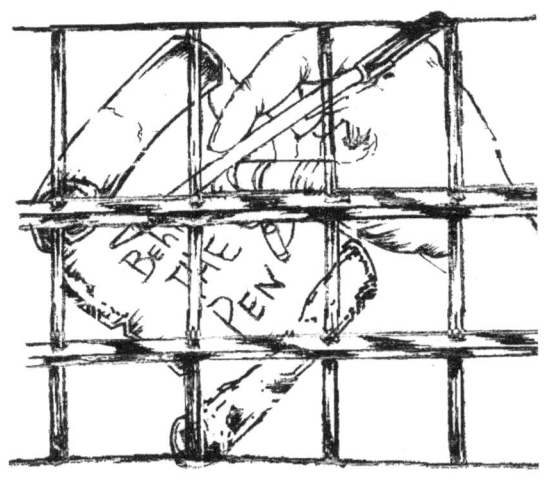

Behind The Pen Publishing LLC presents

SHAWN TAYLOR

STICKIN'&
MOVIN'

This novel is a work of fiction. Any references to real people, events, establishments, or locales are intended only to give the fiction a sense of reality and authenticity. Other names, characters, and incidents occurring in the work are either the product of the author's imagination or are used fictitiously, as those fictionalized events and incidents that involve real persons. Any character that happens to share the name of a person who is an acquaintance of the author, past or present, is purely coincidental and is in no way intended to be an actual account involving that person.

ISBN 10: 0615287956
ISBN 13: 978-0-615-28795-9
Author: Shawn Taylor
Cover concept by www.MarionDesigns.com

Stickin' & Movin': a novel/by Shawn Taylor
For complete Library of Congress Copyright info contact;

Behind The Pen Publishing, LLC
P.O. Box 230239
Jamaica, NY 11423
Website: BehindThePenPublishingLLC.com
www.facebook.com/ShawnBundyTaylor

Why This Book?

Stickin' & Movin' dispels the myths of easy money by painting the classic tale of a thug two steps away from the finish line before all hell breaks loose. It articulates a tale loosely based on the Author's experiences.

Dedication

This book is dedicated to my mother Christine McGriff

From her two sons Shawn Taylor (The Author) and Tracey

Dukes (The Model). Even though you put us through it, we love you no less.

Shawn Taylor would like to hear comments or questions. Please contact him at Behind The Pen Publishing, LLC P.O. Box 230239, Jamaica NY 11423 or email him at ShawnTaylor@BehindThePenPublishingLLC.com or visit www.BehindThePenPublishingLLC.com

ACKNOWLEDGEMENTS

Regina Cole you not only my partner in business, but my partner in life. Words can't even begin to capture how much I love, respect you and care about you. Thank you, you brought back happiness, purpose, love and Taylor to my life. Love & Loyalty Forever.

Celina and Tracey Dukes, the Ying and the Yang: Celina thanks for everything and thank God for your OCD that made this project better than it could have been!

Tracey, my lil brother (The Model) thanks for keeping me in touch with reality.

Tracy Thomas: (Author of 'Family Comes First')
If it wasn't for you, I wouldn't be writing this.
You're good at what you do. Thank you for taking your time to make sure this project came out right, and showing me the vision in full color.

Chico: Regardless of what, you had my back 100%.
Forever loyal, death before dishonor. Family Comes First!
Ha ha ha.

Dre.: You done came up homie, I'm proud of you!! You keep me motivated!! I'm trying to match your hustle.

XL: It's been a long road homie! Thanks for your un-conditional love, support, and loyalty. I don't run across too many real dudes these days. These niggas don't even deserve shout-outs, but you homie, can never be ignored!! E-man: You know you get a shout out. Everything you told me you showed me. Thanks for restoring my faith in niggas again. Much love homie!! Fresh: Thanks for not co-signing my bullshit and always challenging me and helping me grow. Stay focused and I can't wait to read the book. Money: I'm a better person for having met you. Your friendship and guidance mean a lot to me. Thank you for remaining true. Yak and Al: I wish that at your age I could have had the discipline and intelligence that you two have. Stay focused and look forward to bigger things. To Queens: I miss you! You've been so good to me and bad at the same time. Eleven years removed, and I still think about you every day.

R.I.P. Bigga and Black Jason - 112th and Farmers.

Stickin' & Movin':
An Urban Fiction Tale.

Auburn Correctional Facility 2008.

"*I* respect what niggas like 'Preme and Tommy did for the game! I just ain't feeling the way their stories end. The game has evolved. Dudes is sprinkling that legal money on top of they dirty cash."

As usual, Bundy had a captive audience. Although he'd

long ago had his crowd sold on his philosophy, he was really testing his spiel for any flaws. He planned on using the same speech on his small crew of wild bandits that he'd left in the streets prior to his current incarceration. With a mere thirty days left to his conditional release date, Bundy was already setting his mind on a silverback styled corporate takeover of the 'hood.

"My mans Chico, Sosa and 'em be incorporating they shit. The bank will give niggas cars through a corporate fleet rate under their company name, so them niggas be pushing all type of shit. Willie status is no longer judged by if your shit is paid for."

"So basically ya' mans and 'em is fronting." All eyes turned toward Born, as he continued. "They living outside they means, acting like they got it when they don't. That's the shit that'll turn a nigga broke." Born was due to hit the bricks in ninety days, and although he and Bundy were supposed to hook up in the town, Born had 'funny style' ways that bordered on that of a hater.

As much as Born irked Bundy, he'd long ago learned to mask his emotions, as he broke down the math. "That's where you get it twisted Born. Do the math. A CL600 Benz is gonna cost a nigga a buck forty. Why spend that on a toy that's gonna depreciate in value as soon as you pull it off the lot? A true businessman is gonna put ten thou down on it and use the other buck thirty to open up a few businesses. So if those few businesses pull in twenty thou a month, even if the payment is two thou a month on a lease, the bank only sees that a nigga's making eighteen thou a month. So the car is paying for it's self through the businesses."

"Yeah, but a nigga don't own it," Born challenged.

"So what! You get a three year lease, and then trade it in. A real baller is gonna want to upgrade and move on after three years anyway. At least you ain't lost a hundred grand that could've been more useful elsewhere. You gotta treat them shits like the toys they are. The new hustle is having your assets outweigh your liabilities. Under the mattress drug money don't exist as far as the banking institution is concerned."

At that moment, Bundy noticed a dude by the name of U-Majesty cross the Queens court that Bundy and his team occupied. One of Bundy's soldiers named Al-Boogie had given U-Majesty a bundle of dope for his man to move in a cellblock to which Bundy had no access. U-Majesty gave Bundy a brief head nod that caused him to lean over and whisper into Al-Boogie's ear.

"Yo, did the God ever get back to you 'bout that money?

'Cause I'm starting to think that lame is trying to slow walk us since he knows I'm 'bout to touch down soon."

"I hollered at him in the chapel the other day, and I ain't gon' lie, I was starting to get the feeling that ole' boy was giving us the run around." Al-Boogie was hesitant to give Bundy the news, knowing his boy was a loose cannon, and wouldn't think twice about risking his release date to teach U-Majesty a lesson. "You want me to go holler at 'em?"

"Nah, I got this." Bundy wasted no time making his way towards U-Majesty. The crowd parted as Bundy neared. At 6'5" and 250 pounds of solid muscle, Bundy's approach would seem intimidating to the hardest of gangsters. By the time U-Majesty turned, Bundy was within striking distance.

"Bundy! Peace God."

Bundy stared at his outstretched hand, ignoring it, as he smirked, "I done told you a hunned times nigga, I ain't God-body." Bundy leaned into U-Majesty, snarling, "So what's the verdict on that bundle of 'Sleepy-Bags' I gave you?" Bundy could tell by the pause, that U-Majesty was about to hit him with the sob story. Before he could utter a complete sentence, Bundy laid him out with an overhand right.

"Yeah Bundy, what happened was...Before he could

utter a complete sentence, Bundy laid him out with an over hand right." The sound of bone meeting flesh caused the men in the weight pit to turn in their direction. By then, all the spectators saw was U-Majesty flat on his back and Bundy making his way back to the Queens Court.

For the remainder of the rec period, Bundy kept a watchful eye on U-Majesty in the event he got up the courage to strike back. He peeped the older God ask a few of his comrades and allies for a shank, but when they saw him nod towards Bundy as they inquired to his reason, most gave an excuse as to why he'd have to wait. The majority of the older cons that U-Majesty dealt with didn't want problems on the level that Bundy went. His group of wild thugs was posted around their court with bangers up their sleeves and razors ready.

About forty-five minutes later, inmates were lining up for the early return. Bundy's crew flanked his sides, blocking off every possible point of attack, in the event that U-Majesty decided to pull a stunt move. "Boogie, I'll see you in the A.M. son. I'm calling it a night." Bundy bumped fists with Al-Boogie, giving him dap as he locked in his cell.

As soon as Precious got in from work, the first thing she did was kick off her shoes and began rubbing her feet. As simple a task as it was, the act alone always made her wish that her man Bryce was there to rub them for her. *It won't be long girl*, she thought, smiling to herself. Precious never thought she could actually do it, because four years and three months, without her 'Boo-Bear' felt like a lifetime. All of her girlfriends told her she was a fool to sit by idly and wait for a man with all she had going for herself.

She was a legal secretary at the prestigious firm of Solomon, Berry, & Myers. At twenty-five, she had a townhouse she rented right off Union Turnpike behind the Criminal Court building, dental and medical benefits, no kids, and her own car. By any man's standards, Precious was considered a good catch, which is why her girls constantly badgered her concerning her loyalty to Bryce.

Although Precious was well aware of his street name, she couldn't put the beast everyone called Bundy, to her Boo-Bear, Bryce; lucky for Bundy, because Precious had done every last day of his five flat sentence without missing a weekend visit. The sound of her phone ringing put an even bigger smile on her face as she glanced at the clock by the couch. "8:30, Boo-Bear time!" she mumbled, noting Bryce's regular time for calling. It was the one thing she'd come to look forward to. Being that he had an open date, their calls were filled with discussions of the couple's plans upon Bundy's release.

"Hey Boo-Bear!"

The sound of her excitement caused Bundy to crack a huge smile. "Hey baby girl. All that enthusiasm for me?"

"You ain't know?" Precious got right to the subject on her mind. "I got your release outfit." Precious knew this was important to Bryce. Out of all his years, the redundant state greens he was forced to wear in prison was one of his top complaints.

"Okay, so what you got for ya' man?" Bundy's question was two fold. He knew Precious could be frugal, and he respected it, because she lived off a legitimate paycheck. Yet, he also knew he could have easily had one of his homies cop him his 'fit.

"I got you some Omavi jeans, and a v-neck Nostic thermal...that's Jim Jones' new clothing line. I got you some construction Timbs too." Precious knew her man wasn't with the colorful patterns that the younger crowd was into sporting. He always said that true hustlers didn't walk around resembling a box of crayons.

"Yeah, you did good babe."

"Umm hmm! I can't wait to pick you up. That is one ride to Auburn I won't mind taking." Precious laughed, adding, "Gas prices are way up too."

"Whoa, baby girl, I thought we discussed this already? I want to take the bus. You know, give myself a lil' time to think." The phone got silent, which Bryce knew meant only one thing. Precious was pissed. He knew she would automatically assume he was brushing her off so that Chico or Sosa could pick him up. One of her main fears was that Bundy would return to his old ways. Her main reason for thinking so was the fact that he'd never learned to control his violent behavior. His conditional release date only held because his victims were too intimidated to snitch.

"You have got to be kidding me Bryce! You will have plenty of time to..."

Bundy cut Precious off, "How 'bout a compromise babe? You can pick me up from Port Authority. Besides, weren't you just preaching to me 'bout gas prices going up?"

Again, silence, "Fine! I'm not trying to ruin this moment."

"So what's up witchu? How's work?" Bundy tried feeling Precious out.

"Work's fine. Speaking of, what are your plans for work when you get out?"

Although Precious couldn't see him, Bundy shrugged his shoulders. "I dunno. I've been thinking 'bout that. With my record, I'm figuring my only shot left is to run my own business. I can't picture these crackers giving a violent nigga like myself a shot. Shit, I'd probably have them muh'fuckers scared to crack the safe when I'm around." Bundy chuckled, but Precious didn't find his words the least bit amusing.

"Bryce that shit ain't funny! That's the problem right there. You seem to be okay with the fact that you're violent. If you're cool with it, then how do you expect to change it? You have to identify the flaw before you can modify the behavior."

Here we go with that psychology shit, Bundy thought, moving the phone piece away from his ear.

"Are you even listening to me Bryce?" Precious barked, knowing her man all too well.

"I'm here."

"Baby, I ain't trying to preach, but I don't want you trying to do too much too fast. A business takes time. You need capital, discipline, and patience. You may not be able to do that right away. I hope you realize that."

"Yeah," Bundy knew Precious' outlook came from a legitimate standpoint, but with the help of his former crimees, the big man planned on taking a few short cuts.

Precious' voice took on a softer tone, as she coaxed him. "I'm not trying to knock your dreams Bryce, just prepare you for reality. Times are hard out here, and people are struggling. By the looks of the economy, we're heading for a recession. Like I said, gas is up. So are eggs, milk, and oil. I just want to prepare you for the struggle."

"I know babe." The truth of the matter was Bundy didn't give a damn about a recession or gas prices. He'd done close to half a decade daydreaming about V-12 Bentley Coupes. "Precious, I'm gonna have to holler at you tomorrow. We've gotta end this call."

"Okay Boo-Bear. Think about what I said. I love you!"

"I will, and I love you too Babe!

Chapter 2

The Murdock Ave. Crew!

Murdock, 'Sosa Block.

As soon as the triple black 645 BMW convertible pulled onto the block, Yak and O ran up to the window grabbing the work from Sosa. They had run out of drugs about an hour ago. It was becoming a regular routine, and was beginning to frustrate the workers. Sosa had the manpower to handle the traffic that came through

Murdock, but he had two flaws in his character which stagnated his ability to be a good hustler.

For starters, he was greedy. The second problem was that he didn't trust anybody. That included his two lieutenants, Yak and O. He never learned to utilize them fully, and couldn't stand the thought of anyone getting over on him, period! Therefore, he tried to be a one man army, taking on every level of his operation, from copping, cooking, bagging, and even transporting the crack cocaine. Had Sosa possessed an ounce of trust, his daily profits could triple on the busy Murdock Avenue Intersection known as "The Docks."

"What's happening?" Sosa jumped out of his whip, scanning the block for fiends.

"That's what I was just about to ask you, nigga!" Yak barked.

"What the fuck is wrong witchu?" Sosa barked back.

Yak couldn't take it anymore, so he laid his cards on the table. "What the fuck is wrong wit' me? Nigga, you's the one stalling progress." Yak's arms started to get over animated, as he continued, "For every few bundles we move, we gotta wait just as long for yo' ass to come re-up. We got an empty stash house that the soldiers be fucking in, 'cause if task ran through here bustin' the door

down, ain't shit in it for dudes to be worrying 'bout."
Yak pointed towards the second story window above the
bodega, where they used a crack head's apartment as their
makeshift headquarters. His actions caused Sosa to scope
out the area, in the event Yak was tipping off some nearby
undercovers to their stash spot. Seeing his distrust, Yak
got even more agitated.

Unbeknown to Sosa, Yak had gotten plenty of offers
from other dealers around the way to hustle for the opposing
team. Some even offered Yak weight on consignment,
subtly suggesting that in the event of 'Sosa demise, a real
hustler could pull Murdock up to its full potential. Yak's
loyalty was slowly starting to weaken.

Seeing the situation on the verge of getting out of
hand, O decided to step in to get 'Sosa focus off of Yak's
rambling. "You know how Yak gets Sosa, and I don't
blame him. I risk my freedom for the money, and you half
stepping. I wish you'd stay out here for just one whole
day, so you can see how much dough you be losing doing
it your way." O's approach was a bit more diplomatic, as
usual.

"If we bullshitting lemme know Sosa, 'cause I can
do better than this hustling for dolo off the hip," Yak
continued. He was referring to the method most of

Queen's hustlers were resorting to in the new millennium. Some called it a "paper route;" others nicknamed the system "hustling off the hip;" some just a plain old "we will deliver motto" yet, the gist of his reference implied the same across the board. Like New York's real estate market, space in the Rotten Apple was limited. Owning a drug block was a luxury. Yak felt Sosa didn't fully capitalize off, and therefore did not deserve.

Sosa on the other hand, didn't even bother to get into it with Yak. He knew the young gunner had made a valid point. Sosa also knew Yak was well aware of his trust issues. It was only a matter of time before his whole clique would be wondering why they were struggling under a boss who seemed to be no more than a half hearted hustler. *A tribe is only as good as their leader*, thought Sosa. He chose his next words carefully.

"Yak, O, I'm gon' keep it real with ya'll. I've been half stepping, for the most part. I'm waiting for Bundy to come home and basically take up the slack in the areas I lack. I owe that much to him." Sosa put up a good front. He only meant half of what he said; the other half was him using Bundy's influence over the Murdock Ave. posse as the glue to hold his team together a little bit longer. "Gimme a few weeks Yak and things will get better. That's my word!"

Bundy's name sparked a glimmer of hope to Yak's dilemma. Yak was too much of an opportunist to ignore 'Sosa promise. Yak knew Bundy was probably the only man in their clique who would come home with a hunger that could match his own.

Since Yak seemed content, O decided to switch subjects. "Yo Sosa! Guess who came through the block stuntin' in that new Audi R8?" O didn't even give him a chance to guess, shouting out, "That nigga Chico doing it big Son! He said to come by the club so he can holler atch'u 'bout some thangs."

"He ain't say nothing else?"

"Nah, Son had a bad lil' bitch wit' him too." Yak had the block back bubbling in a matter of minutes.

Sosa sat atop a milk crate leaning against the front of the bodega. He pulled out his cell phone and immediately got Chico on the phone. "Yo, it's Sosa. I got your message. What's good?"

"You nigga, that's what. When is the soonest you can stop by the lounge? I need to rap witchu for a few."

"I'ma stop through tonight around nine. I gotta discuss something with you too."

"Nine it is. See you then." And just that quick, Chico

hung up.

Sosa knew the drill. He was well aware of Chico's contempt for talking business over the phone.

"Damn!" He stared at the phone while shaking his head. *Guess I'll find out tonight at nine*, he thought, turning his attention to the traffic coming to and from Murdock.

Just then, a crackhead named Angie walked up on him. Sosa and Angie had gone to Andrew Jackson H.S. back when she was the head cheerleader for the football team. Since then, her addiction had withered away the looks that once had half the boys in her school vying for her attention. All that was left of her now was a disheveled shell of the dime piece that once was.

"Sosa, can I get a favor?"

"If it's credit forget it. I'm trying to run a business Ang."

"Lemme get a twenty Sosa? I got you when I get my check." Sosa already had her Welfare card as collateral off her last plea for credit.

"C'mon Sosa..." Before she could continue, one of the workers named Pee-Wee gave Angie an offer.

"I got a twenty for some head," then looked at Sosa for approval.

Sosa shrugged his shoulders, stating nonchalantly, "It's

coming out your pay, so make it worth ya' while."

Pee-Wee glanced up at the stash house, giving Angie a look as if to say, 'So what's up?' Angie broke fool.

"What? You crab ass niggas trying to play me? All you niggas combined couldn't buy this pussy, let alone to kiss my ass!"

Pee-Wee laughed, as he pointed at her feet. "Bitch please! Yo Sosa, look at the bitch feet..." Sosa always told lil' Pee-Wee that if a woman had bad feet, then chances were she neglected other parts of her body. Based on that, Pee-Wee started getting wreck on Angie "...and the bitch got the nerve to be wearing sandals."

"Fuck you, nigga! You the one trying to get some," Angie struck back, defending what little pride she had left.

"Them ain't sandals Pee-Wee. That's her dry ass feet looking like old leather," another worker chimed in.

All they did while hustling was snap on the less fortunate addicts that came through the block on a regular basis. Angie didn't stand a chance against one of them, let alone all of them.

"Last time I seen feet that ashy, Godzilla was crushing Tokyo wit em," another youth cracked causing laughter to drown out her retort.

"Her feet look like her ex-pimp's gators."

By now the crew was doubled over in laughter. All
Angie could do was throw them the middle finger as she
eased her way off the strip.

"And don't come back 'till you ready to give my lil'
man some head...Bee yotch!!!"

"Squa-leee," Yak shouted, business as usual. At the
warning, the workers stashed their packs, but the patrol
car zoomed past them without so much as a second glance.

Sosa leaned back on the crate and cracked open a bottle
of Mystic as the day continued on. "Just another day on
the strip" he mumbled, tilting his fitted Yankee hat over
his eyes to block out the sun.

The Player's Lounge-Lennox Ave.,
Harlem N.Y. 9:00pm.

The Player's Lounge was an after hour's club that
catered to the city's underworld major figures. It was
more so an illegal gambling hole / underground hideaway
where the more affluent criminals hung out to politic and

network. A wiretap in the lounge would probably net the Feds over a hundred indictments easily. Lucky for the dwellers of this luxurious ghetto dungeon, the men that ran the spot were stand-up dudes.

The Player's Lounge was the brainchild of DJ Deuce, a Queen's native who had become one of the leading figures in the mixtape CD game. Since Deuce's rise to the top of the game was based on the ability to get exclusive freestyles from hip-hop's elite, he'd met and rubbed elbows with some of New York's biggest and brightest ballers. It was then that he decided to open a club that catered strictly to them, a place where they didn't have to worry about getting pat frisked for weapons, or have less fortunate players plotting on their pockets. Since Deuce was too busy to run the club due to his popularity in music, he recruited his longtime friend and road dawg, Chico to run the spot for him. Even with Chico skimming off the top, the Player's Lounge pulled in so much of a profit that Deuce never noticed a discrepancy in the books.

Sosa actually loved it when Chico summoned him to the Player's Lounge. Just being amongst so many street legends and gangsters had Sosa feeling like a made man. Being that the club was located in Harlem, Sosa opted for the 'Bird Gang' look. He strutted through the entrance decked out in Gucci; sneakers, jeans, and a black leather baseball jacket with the trademark green and red stripes adorning everything. He even bit off their style by sporting a Gucci scarf over his Gucci fitted cap. He would have never guessed that the double takes from most of the female patrons at the Player's Lounge were based on the opinion that his matching ensemble was overkill.

"Chico's downstairs in the back office," one of the burly bouncers informed him. "He's waiting on you."

Sosa made his way to the office, and as soon as he entered, he was greeted by Chico with open arms.

"My big head nigga Sosa!" Chico smiled. At 5"9' and 175 pounds, Chico was considered a pretty boy by most women's standards. He had silky waves that did a complete 360 around the crown of his head. Although he was of mixed heritage, his Puerto Rican heritage showed more than his African American side. Sosa was more of a short and stocky brawler type whose almond complexion was still two shades darker than Chico's.

"Have a seat. You just in time." Chico released Sosa from his embrace.

"I don't have much time." Chico checked the time on his Platinum Rolex Masterpiece. "I was wondering if you heard from our nigga, Bundy?"

Sosa shook his head indicating that he hadn't.

"Yeah, well don't feel bad, 'cause neither have I. I was just trying to get a feel of where his mind might be so I can come at him with the best offer, but I want to keep his interest at heart, ya' feel me?"

Sosa nodded, but internally he wanted to laugh. He was well aware of the story behind Bundy's five year sentence, and knew that Chico had played a major part in the big man getting knocked. Although Chico had gone out of his way to make sure Bundy was financially straight during his bid, he had no way of knowing how Bundy was going to come at him now that his day of freedom was around the corner.

"I'm in a position to help my nigga eat, and I don't know what route to go."

Sosa could tell that Chico looked stumped, as he continued on.

"I mean, should I cop him a whip, some jewels, or just set him out wit' straight cash?" Usually Chico's questions were rhetorical, but this time, he actually waited on Sosa to provide him with an answer.

"He ain't never went there wit' me Chico, but if I had to guess, I'd go with straight cash. A nigga can't go wrong with that." Chico nodded as if he agreed.

"You should still offer the man a way to make some paper on a daily basis, that way you'd actually be giving him something he couldn't put a price on." The voice belonged to Gooch. He was named after the anonymous bully on the 80's sitcom 'Different Strokes'. He moved in the same manner as the character on the show seldom seen, and seldom heard. He was the head of security at the Player's Lounge.

"I could always use some extra muscle on the team. From what I hear, Bundy don't seem like the type to mind putting in a lil' work." Gooch smirked.

"Sounds good Gooch. I just want to have a few suggestions to throw his way, and then hopefully he'll choose one." Chico turned to Sosa who seemed to be in deep thought.

"Before you leave, I'll have Gooch secure that package for you." Sosa tossed Gooch his car keys. The package Chico was referring to was the cocaine he supplied Yak and O with. Chico was also 'Sosa connect.

"I was gonna offer Bundy a position on the block. Just let him oversee things. So I might be doubling up soon."

The idea seemed to please Chico, "Word? That's what's up, a lot of lil' moves. At least he's eating, a thou here, a few thou there."

Gooch got up and disappeared through the back door of Chico's office. Sosa knew that was his cue to excuse himself. As he closed the door behind him, he made his way to the entertainment section of the Lounge. He was pleased to see that he walked in to the middle of a comedian doing his act. The comedian was a skinny white kid called Paulie G. Sosa had seen his act before and knew the crowd was in for a treat. Re-up was 'Sosa favorite part of the night because he actually got to mingle with the upper echelon of ghetto celebs, even if it was only for a brief moment, and at a distance. Sosa ordered a shot of Hennessy as he watched Paulie G through the club's stage lights.

"By a show of hands, how many of ya'll think Bush is the worst President, America has ever had?" Practically every hand in the club went up. Paulie G zeroed in on a patron who didn't hold his hand up. "What? Big Man, I know you ain't feeling Bush, is you?"

The man shrugged his shoulders as if he was at a loss for words. Paulie G took it as his cue to go in on the man.

"I understand Big Guy. The closest you come to politics is the latest issue of Don Diva." The crowd started to chuckle. "Biggie, you've gotta stay up on ya' poll tricks babe. That muh'fucka Bush got me pushing a Toyota

Scion!" The crowd started snickering. "I gotta crack open the sunroof just to drive down the block." Paulie G walked slowly across the stage shaking his head, while mumbling in disgust. "Damn near charging my broke ass twenty grand to push an aluminum square go-cart. Ain't that some shit!"

All of a sudden Paulie's head popped up, and with watery eyes, he spazzed on the crowd, "Weapons of mass destruction my ass! At least admit we trying to extort some oil outta Habib and 'em. If I'm doing a jux, let me know it's a robbery dammit!" His rant was followed by a series of applause as he took a seat on his stool and a sip of Remy Red.

"Any of ya'll got peoples overseas in the armed forces?" Half of the hands in the club went up.

"Yeah, I feel your pain." Paulie G started nodding. "I was a Marine over in Desert Storm." Again, the patrons applauded. Paulie G jumped off the stool, yelling, "Fuck is ya'll clapping for? That shit fucked me up! If ya'll was there ya'll wouldn't be clapping. That ain't no place for a skinny dude like me to be."

Paulie G began to pick his nose as he started in on one of his infamous war stories.

"I 'member this one time they had us jumping outta

planes, right? Now, I'm scared of heights. I didn't put that on my application, 'cause I was just trying to get the government to pay for my college education. Anyway, so my D.I. that stands for drill instructor, 'cause they're instructed to drill my ass every chance they get." A few chuckles went around the room as Paulie got back to his story. "Anyway, my D.I. screams, Dammit soldier, you done snuck to the back of the line, but it's the end of the line for you now. If you don't jump out of this plane right now, I'm gonna get this big black Mandingo Sergeant to bend you over and fuck you dead in your ass!"

Paulie mimicked the drill instructor by standing in a bowlegged stance; spit flying from his mouth as he yelled until he turned beet red. He then switched places, pretending to be that soldier again. He took his palm and did a long exaggerated swipe across his face from his forehead to his chin, flicking his fingers as if he was removing the spit from his face.

At that moment, a heckler from the crowd yelled out, so Paulie, did you jump?"

Paulie paused for a second before answering. "Yeah! A little at first," grabbing his buttocks for emphasis. The crowd roared with laughter.

The Gooch appeared at Sosa table, leaned into his ear

and whispered. Once he left, Sosa took a final sip of his drink, adjusted the napkin on his table and slipped his car keys into his pocket before exiting the Players Lounge.

As he pulled off in his Beemer, Sosa daydreamed the perfect fantasy. Bundy; running Murdock Ave. while he rubbed elbows with the hustlers in the Players Lounge on his quest for Boss status.

Chapter 3

Bundy's Home!

Three weeks later...

$\mathscr{T}$he funny thing about prison is its ability to play tricks on the mind. Once Bundy boarded the bus for Port Authority, it was as if it had been the day after his arrest. The air in the free world actually felt different to his lungs, and the four years and three months he'd just completed seemed like nothing more than a memory. He immediately sought out the back row seat in the far corner of the bus. Once he got comfortable, he adjusted his hat over his eyes and began to zone out his surroundings.

His thoughts drifted to his Q-Borough brethrens. 'Hood legends like Tommy Montana, Supreme, Black Jus', and The Corley's had made their mark in history, whether through corrections, the casket, or opting for retirement. Bundy, like the rest of the new generation, planned on taking the reins, rotating their fifteen minutes of fame as if it were phone time on Riker's Island.

The new regime was full of young entrepreneurs such as Rob, Lo, DJ Clue, and The Black Hand Movement. Although Bundy respected the ingenuity of these legitimate businessmen, he felt his only option was to take a few much needed short cuts. Between Chico and the Players Lounge, and his influence on DJ Deuce, Bundy felt they could accomplish the same type of network as the ballers around the way, even if it was on a smaller scale. *Gotta start somewhere nigga. We gonna crawl before we walk.* He figured all the pieces were in place, he just wasn't there to lead them in the direction his prison daydreams wanted his crew to go.

"Fuck that! Chico owe," he mumbled as he got a few z's while the bus made its way towards New York City.

The last thing on his mind was the very reason he felt Chico owed him.

Once upon a time...

"Stickin' and movin,' that's what we's about, Chico! Ain't no need to complicate this shit. We don't know shit about this dude, so go in hard and fast." Bundy checked the chamber of his Ruger P89, and cocked back the slide, while Chico nodded. He held the Walther PK tightly in his hand hoping Bundy didn't notice his nerves were on edge.

"You sure this shit is worth it?" Chico asked. Chico could hear Yak suck his teeth from the back seat of the car and ignored it. *Easy for you to cop an attitude, you get to stay out here.*

Yak had the luxury of being the getaway driver, and Chico silently wished it was him doing the driving.

On their way toward the side of the house, Bundy grabbed Chico by the arm, reminding him, "Don't forget, when we're clear, toss the gun!" It was the one rule Bundy lived by. Without a gun, he figured if they were pulled over the three of them had a fighting chance at a trial.

They had followed a white couple in a Jaguar from a night on the town back to their home in Sag Harbor, Long Island. Bundy knew Chico wasn't the type to do home invasions. He didn't possess that aggressive mean streak that he and Yak had inherited. The sole purpose for his participation was the fact that he used to burglarize homes back in the late nineties and knew a lot about home security systems.

The trio was working off of pot luck when they decided to try the couple at hand. Chico crept into the back yard and opened up the box that powered the home's alarm system, cutting the red wire that beaded its independent power source. Just then, their dog had crept up on Chico and began barking. Out of nowhere, Bundy crept up on the bulldog and snapped its neck. When Chico heard the dog's final yelp, he looked up to see Bundy with all his weight on the dog, its head shifted at a grotesque angle. Chico was already scared of Bundy, but the sight made him even more uncomfortable.

"It's done," he told Bundy, closing the box. Before Chico could go over the plan one last time with him, the behemoth sized Bundy lifted his foot and kicked the door down in one hard motion. By the time the owners of the house realized what was going on, Bundy and Chico had them face down on their living room floor at gunpoint.

"I'ma say this one time, 'cause we ain't got all day to be bullshitting wit' ya'll. Where's the cash?"

"My wallets in my back pocket," the man told Bundy. He was a silver haired gentleman that looked to be in his early fifties. The wife had a mane of grey hair and had definitely aged gracefully. Bundy tucked his gun in the waistband of his pants, and savagely ripped off the man's back pocket, stuffing the cash into his own.

"I appreciate it Ole' Timer, but that's just the tip of the iceberg. Now, where's the real dough?"

"That's it, but my checkbook is in..." Bundy punched the man in the back of his head. He didn't really want to hurt the man, but even his subtle attack felt harsh to the senior. Bundy didn't realize that invading their home was traumatizing enough. Regardless of the fact, he tried to violate them in a civilized manner. He decided to change tactics, figuring that the man might have cared more for his wife's well being than his own. Bundy pulled his gun on her.

"Mirar, Joey DeBarge!" He called out to Chico, using an alias, but also trying to be funny. "Go upstairs and check the rest of el casa." Chico flipped him the bird, as Bundy turned his attention back to the couple.

"This is ya'll last warning. Where's the money? And think before you answer, 'cause if I don't like what I hear, I'm blowing your bitch's brains all over this expensive carpet ya'll got."

"Please young man. I'm telling you the truth." It was then that Bundy noticed the wife lift her head up, and caught the disgusted look she gave her husband. Bundy took it to mean the older man had chosen his stash over his wife.

At that moment, Chico sweetened the pot by coming down the stairs with the couple's daughter in tow. "Yo Sugar Bear, look what I found." Chico smiled, getting Bundy back for the DeBarge comment. Bundy guessed the girls age to be about twenty.

"Well lookie here!" Bundy looked at the parents, then to the daughter. He decided to bluff them by raising the sixteen shot Ruger towards the girl. "Looks to me like ya'll lil' girl just sweetened the pot. Now, this is my last time asking. Where the fuck is the moolah?"

"I beg of you, please don't hurt my child. I have a box of jewelry upstairs in the walk-in closet in our bedroom." Before he could finish, Chico had already made his way to the bedroom to relieve the couple of their jewels. Bundy wasn't budging; he continued to press the issue of a safe.

"I'm not as thirsty as my cohort, so, one last time..."
He cocked back the hammer on the Ruger as he held the
daughter by the arm. At that moment, the wife couldn't
take it anymore. Bundy didn't even see the lightning,
fast slap she delivered to her husband as she screamed,
"Enough Paul! Give them the money. It's bad enough I
wasn't good enough reason, but I can't believe you're
willing to risk our daughter's life."

She looked up at Bundy. "It's behind the picture frame
in the room we use for business. It's the third door to your
left. The combination is, 34 left, 22 right, 18 left."

"Louisa, for all we know they are going to kill us
anyway." Paul tried to justify his actions.

Bundy cuffed the family, went to the room and found
what he was after. He found a small Jansport knapsack
in the daughter's room, and used it to stash the cash. He
stuffed ten thousand in his jeans, figuring Chico was in
the next room doing the same with the jewels. By the time
they exited the house, Yak had already started the car and
got them back to Jamaica, Queens in record time. They
divided the jewelry, but Bundy informed them that the
cash would have to wait until they got to his crib.

"Gimme your gun Chico." Chico passed him the gun
as he pulled up to a sewer and threw it in. Unbeknownst

to Bundy, Chico had a small glock backup hidden in the small of his back. He was so leery of Bundy and Yak trying to play him, he kept the equalizer a secret.

With the money and jewelry safely tucked away in the trunk of the car, Bundy figured they were clear, so he instructed Yak to take them to the store. As soon as they pulled to the curb, a blue and white patrol car pulled up behind them.

"Just be cool," Bundy mumbled. Chico quietly shifted, and slid the small glock auto underneath Yak's seat. The cop jumped out of the car and ran into the bodega to get some grub for a late night snack. "Whew!" They wound up skipping their store run, and made their way toward Murdock instead.

After counting, and tucking away the proceeds they all decided to go see one of Bundy's chicks. As soon as they reached Murdock Avenue, Tina popped her head out the window. "Bundy, don't even get out of that car if you ain't got no liqs." Bundy looked at Yak and knew this was going to be one of those freaky nights. A successful 'jux' was like Viagra to the two of them, so Bundy quickly volunteered to get the liquor. He jumped in the car so fast Chico barely got the words out.

"Bundy, hol' up." But Bundy had already peeled off.

Chico didn't know how he was going to explain the gun under the seat anyway. He'd broken one of Bundy's golden rules, and was in no hurry to admit it. That night, no more than fifteen minutes later, Bundy parked in front of the liquor store and when he came out had a bag full of spirits. As he opened the door, a cop approached him and his partner pulled up blocking him in.

"I hope you aren't on your second round and driving young man?" Bundy knew everything was straight, so he didn't panic nor get defensive. He put the liquor on the passenger seat, as the cop stepped towards the open door.

"No sir. I'll do the drinking once I'm at my lady's crib and I'll be spending the night." The cop shined his flashlight at the floor looking for empty beer cans and that's when he spotted the gun.

"Gun!" He quickly drew his weapon as his partner flanked Bundy's left side. The next thing Bundy knew, he was getting his rights read to him as the officer secured the cold hard steel against his wrists. "You have the right to remain silent. Anything you say..."

"Last stop, Port Authority!" the driver yelled. At the same time, Bundy jolted out of his sleep. For the last four years and three months, he had the same recurring dream of the night of his arrest. Every time he had the dream, he woke up the moment they put the handcuffs on him. He took that as a sign. He vowed that he would never return to prison…not because he was never going to commit another crime, but because if he ever found himself boxed in again, he swore to go out like Larry Davis, in a blaze of glory. Unlike Larry, Bundy was going to shoot it out to the death.

As soon as his feet hit the pavement of New York City, he bellowed, "Bundy's home!"

Chapter 4
Bishop Takes Pawn

"*Miss*, I'm sorry, but you are going to have to move your vehicle." This was the second traffic cop to warn Precious. She silently wondered why Bryce didn't just allow her to pick him up from Auburn like she planned to. For years she pictured the day they released her Boo-Bear from the dank stone prison. Her day was going nothing like she'd envisioned it on all those occasions.

"I was told that I can't park in the street. Now you're telling me I can't park here. Where am I supposed to park?" Precious had her Toyota Corolla idling across the street from the Port Authority at the mouth of the parking lot that doubled as the tour guide buses headquarters.

"I don't know ma'am, but if you stay here I'm going to be forced to write you a ticket." The traffic cop was supposed to have written the ticket long ago, but the petite caramel coated dime piece had him awestruck. Precious began to plead to the traffic cop for a few more seconds of waiting time.

"If I could get fifteen more minutes, I'm sure..." Precious began squinting in the direction of Port Authority, causing the traffic cop to look in the same direction. That's when she saw him.

"Bryce!" Precious hopped out of her Corolla and started waving in Bundy's direction. The crowd seemed to part for the mammoth sized ex-con. Precious jumped into his arms as Bundy swung her around once before dropping her back to her feet. The traffic cop couldn't help but glance at her round firm ass, wondering how someone so petite could posses so much junk in her trunk. "Damn!" he mumbled. He walked off as the two of them got in the car and made their way toward Queens.

"So what do you want to do first?" Bundy smiled. He kept glancing back at Precious every few minutes, proud to be able to call such a specimen of beauty his lady.

"I wanna do a lil' shopping. You brought that for me?" Precious pulled out a knot of bills and handed them to him. Bundy counted out five grand, as Precious began nagging him about it.

"I don't know why you need that much money to go shopping Bryce. That kind of money should be kept in a bank. You could get robbed walking around with that amount of cash." Bundy looked at her like she was crazy. He wished a nigga even dreamed about trying to rob him. *They better kill me.* He knew better than to say it aloud.

Forty minutes later, Precious was parking her Toyota on the roof of the Coliseum's parking area. Their first stop was S&D's. Bundy had nearly half a decade worth of no fashion sense, but he knew whatever S&D carried, it was bound to be the latest styles on the streets.

"May I help you?" Bundy noticed the cutie soliciting him. The sales girls at the boutique were all top-notch honies. Bundy figured it must have been a job requirement. Precious instantly got jealous, but let her man have his moment.

"That depends. Do you get a commission?" The girl nodded. "In that case, stay close by, 'cause you 'bout to do all right for yourself." Bundy shopped just like a man. He grabbed everything that he felt looked good on him, tried it on, and then put it in the salesgirl's arms for purchase. Twenty minutes later, they left the store, and Bundy took Precious to the Jamaican restaurant next to Montego Bay where they dined on rice and peas and oxtails. Bundy grabbed himself a peanut punch as they strolled into Montego Bay where he purchased a pair of black leather Timbs, black Nike ACG's, and some black suede Timbs. "I'm good!" he said, as the couple made their way home.

"I should be back in a few weeks. I just wanna see if it's what they say it is, before I jump out the window without a parachute. They say a nigga can damn near make five thousand off an 'onion' out there." Sosa was talking about Columbus, Ohio. His man Mikey told him the whole town was a gold mine for the right person. Sosa felt he was the dude to deliver. He was willing to step out of character for once, and trust not only Mikey's word, but Yak and O to run the block in his absence. Although Yak held his composure, he was elated to finally have a stash house that actually had something stashed in it.

Sosa had gotten Chico to front him half a key.

Normally, Chico got leery anytime one of his peoples went up on quantity. When Sosa explained the out of town move, Chico reasoned that if he wasn't going to help Sosa eat, then he had to respect the fact that he'd try and get it the best way he knew how.

When Bundy took off his shirt, Precious was pleased with what she saw. All those years of excruciating prison workouts had Bundy looking like a chiseled Greek Adonis. She immediately started kissing and licking his chest. From the ferocity of her passion, Bundy could tell that she hadn't been unfaithful to him during his bid. Precious locked onto his neck like a pitbull in heat, as she palmed his ass and made her way to his belly button. Bundy pointed his pelvis off the bed, as his manhood stood at attention waiting to be serviced. Precious licked all around him but never got to please him in the way he wanted. Bundy tried to guide her head towards his penis, and that's when she set the record straight.

"Uh uh Bryce. You know I don't like doing that." Ever since their days in high school, Precious had never given into Bryce's pleas for oral sex. On more than one occasion he had to find a willing female who would keep their indiscretions on the low. Bundy flipped Precious around and began eating her out as if he was possessed by the devil.

"Umm hmm! Yes Daddy, do that shit!" Precious purred. Bundy felt like a fair exchange was no robbery. He actually resented the fact that his woman's conscience didn't allow her to see that she was being selfish. For that, Bundy reasoned he was going to punish the pussy. He threw Precious forward as she giggled at his rough housing as playfulness. He scooted up on the bed, and entered her warm tight tunnel.

In a matter of a few strokes, Bundy was pounding away. Precious tried to back up off him, but he grabbed her by the waist and continued plowing into her with long hard thrusts. The sound of flesh smacking against her ass, had Precious wet, but in pain. She started talking in tongues, surprising even Bundy with her foul mouth. "Oh gawd, yes! Tear this pussy up, you big dick wilder beast! Oh damn! Shift that uterus Mandingo! Beat it! Beat it! Owww!"

Bundy was smacking her ass until it glowed red. He stuck his thumb so far up her ass, Precious thought she was in a three way gang bang. Bundy figured if she'd let him fuck her in such a fashion, she shouldn't be so inhibited when it came to oral and anal sex. The thought caused him to grind into her to the hilt, as he stroked her with grinding circular motions.

"Yes! Right there! Right there! I'm cumming!" He felt Precious shudder for a few minutes, but he wasn't done yet. He planned on letting her feel every day of his nearly five years of pent up frustration.

He flipped her onto her back, grabbed a handful of ass and began long dicking her while in the missionary position. The hornier she got the more he eased his finger into her ass. He bit into her nipple as she started to squirm and buck back. Bryce loved the fact that he was able to bring his lady multiple orgasms. After about twenty minutes of intense fucking, Precious was pleading with Bryce, "Please Boo-Bear. No more. The dick is too big. It hurts so good."

By then Bryce had her legs around his shoulders and was standing as he dropped her onto his dick, smacking the ass every time she landed on it. He pushed her against the wall, snarling, "Arrgh! I'm cumming!" He damn near pushed Precious through the wall as she squealed for mercy.

When Bundy came out of the shower, he wasn't

surprised to see Precious sound asleep. He went into the bathroom to get dressed, and as he looked into the mirror, he grabbed his dick, "We still got it nigga!" He grabbed the keys to Precious' Toyota, and made his way to Murdock.

Yak was barely paying attention when the Toyota Corolla came cruising down the block. He was so busy keeping an eye on the traffic, he didn't even see Bundy grinning at him through the light tinted windows. Bundy made a right turn and parked the car down the side street, and decided to walk the rest of the way. He didn't want Precious' car to get recognized in a drug area because he'd been away a while and had no idea if Yak or Sosa had any enemies that would be willing to go the lengths he'd been known to. He didn't need anyone mistaking him for their connect, or have any other unforeseen mishaps.

He also wanted to surprise his homie. He hadn't seen Yak since the night of his arrest. As he turned the corner, he jumped out, and this time he was the one surprised. Yak was gone, and in front of him sat an empty crate. "Where the fuck...?" Bundy was stumped, that is, until Yak came out from the shadows of an enclave next to the bodega.

"Well, I'll be damned. My nigga Bundy!" Yak was cheesing, as he stuffed his gun back in the garbage can and walked up to embrace his crimee.

"I see you've still got it, huh? On point like a muh' fucker, a nigga never could creep up on your lil' ass."

"Actually, my lookout hit me on the chirp of your arrival." Yak nodded towards the second story window, as Bundy asked, "Chirped you? Whatch'u mean?"

"Oh yeah, I forgot, you been gone for a minute." Yak pulled out his Nextel phone, hitting the side button. That's when Bundy heard the chirping sound.

"Yo E, don't sweat it. This is my peoples."

"Yeah, I kinda figured that part out," E chirped back.

Yak began to explain, "The Nextel sort of doubles as a walkie talkie, ya' know?" Bundy nodded, as Yak pulled out a second crate and the two began catching up on the 'hood's current events.

"So Chico's tight ass finally gave up the block, huh?" Bundy took a quick inventory of the workers, trying his best to estimate their daily take. "I'm glad he gave it to you Yak. You deserve it."

Yak started shaking his head, as his face showed his disdain. "That nigga ain't give me shit! Faggot ass nigga gave the block to Sosa. He just happens to be outta town at the moment." And as an afterthought, Yak threw in, "I guess I remind Chico too much of that embarrassing stunt he pulled. He probably figured our history ain't go wit' his new image. The shit that gets me tight is the fact that I've always kept our business amongst us. Sosa ain't even running this shit right, son."

"You had your cut of the jux. Why you ain't open up shop with that?" Bundy was talking about the ten thousand they'd all gotten from the robbery that got him his bid, the same ten thousand that Precious had given him half of already.

"I copped a lil' BMW X5. Next thing I know, Jigga done labeled them shits for baby moms only! You know that nigga's word is law. Look what he did to the 4.0's. He killed Range Rover's sales on the smaller engine models. Me, I ain't had a decent come up since you left. I was scared I'd get knocked and be on my way to the Pen as you were coming out. I ain't trying to miss the mother lode, 'cause I know you got some shit planned."

It wasn't a question, and Bundy's smile told Yak that he couldn't be closer to the truth. "Sosa was talking 'bout letting you run the block so he could expand. That would be a good look, 'cause I don't think his heart is in it anymore. Ever since Deuce plugged Chico into the

Player's Lounge, the Docks ain't good enough for Sosa. He wants to be in them niggas league. He wanna look like he moves weight, and just lounges back while his cash is made for him. I guess that's where we supposed to come in."

Bundy interceded with the quickness. "Sosa got it twisted then son, 'cause I want mine like, yesterday! I don't have the time nor patience to sit around here turning ten to twenty, and twenty to a hunned, and a hunned to a gee. I'm just looking to stick up the muh'fucker that done did all that grinding already."

Yak and Bundy gave each other 'dap', as Yak dropped a jewel on the big man. "I feel you my nigga, but never turn down any free cash. Besides I've got a feeling we can turn this thing around in our favor."

"I'm listening."

"You may not be into the hustling, but I am. Since you want the mother lode, and I need a come up, we can work together. Let Sosa offer you the position, then I'll get the freedom to run this shit the way it's supposed to be run."

Bundy thought about it, and realized that Yak had already begun planning for his release. "Damn, you got it all figured out already, huh, planned my shit out for me and what not?" Bundy laughed.

Then Yak hit him with some even more interesting news. "Shit, according to Sosa, he, Chico, and Gooch got your future all planned out. I just know you better than that, so I'm trying to get you to capitalize instead of guerilla pimping them!"

Bundy had to admit, Yak was thinking strategically. It made him take heed to the advice. "Listen, won't you take a ride over to the Player's Lounge with me? I wanna see what Chico and Deuce is working wit'!"

"So this is it, huh? The infamous Player's Lounge! Doesn't look like much," Bundy stated.

"It's underground for the most part. The gambling is illegal, and the liquor license is for the front part only. Members have access to the annex part of the club, and that's where the real money is made."

"C'mon Yak. I wanna hear just how much brainstorming our good friend Chico has been doing when it comes to my future and financial freedom." Bundy and Yak got out of Precious' car and made their way toward the entrance of the club. That's when one of the bouncers stuck his hand out and stopped them.

"I'm gonna need to see a membership card gentlemen." Bundy sized up the cat at the door. The bouncer waited patiently as if he was giving Bundy the chance to decide if he could take him. Bundy admired the fact that the doorman wasn't the least bit intimidated and figured Chico must have gotten himself the best security money could buy. Yak was the one who uttered the magic words.

"Tell Chico Yak is at the door and I brought Bundy to see him." The bouncer spoke into the same system that Yak used on his Nextel, and a moment later, he and Bundy were allowed access.

Gooch was the first to meet them as they entered the Lounge. "Heard a lot about you fam." Gooch shook Bundy's hand with a firm grip that matched his own. Bundy was impressed. He wasn't used to seeing men his size. Yet, so far, every bouncer in the Player's Lounge seemed to be cut from the same mold as him.

Gooch was decorated in jailhouse tattoos that seemed to tell the rest of his story. He escorted Bundy to Chico's office, and upon entry, Chico greeted Bundy with an over exaggerated bear hug. "Big muh'fucking Bundy! Man, it's been a while playboy." He released Bundy at arm's length to get a better look at him. He also tried to read his expression, trying to gauge if the big man held any ill feelings towards him. He could detect none. Gooch stood on the outside reading the body language of both Bundy and Yak.

"Sit down." Chico pointed to the two chairs in front of his desk. "Gooch, get on the horn fa' me, and have our best champagne sent down." As Gooch disappeared, Chico began talking a mile a minute. "I wish you would've told me you were coming. I would've thrown a lil' get together or something."

"I'd rather have it like this Chico. Nice and quiet, ya' know, nothing too big and fancy." Bundy leaned in, whispering, "I'll tell you why in a minute." Bundy grinned, letting Chico ponder the meaning of his statement. His plan was to keep Chico off balance so that when he cracked for his just due, Chico would feel so relieved he wouldn't dare dream of protesting.

"I was telling Bundy 'bout 'Sosa visit with ya'll, and what he planned, I told him he ain't even have to go through all that because according to "Sosa you've got "em covered."

Bundy interrupted. "Yeah, according to Sosa, you've got me covered. So what's the plan daddy-o?"

"Damn B, you ain't wasting no time, huh?"

"Actually, I wasted almost half a decade."

"Yeah, about that..."

Bundy held his hand up, silencing Chico. "Fuck' it! What's done is done. As long as you can help me out I'll hold that bid down like the soldier I am. But I ain't gonna lie, I need you to show me that love and support Sosa was talking 'bout, or I'm bound to move like one of those bitter convicts you read about in them Urban Fiction novels."

"I feel you dawg." Although Chico laughed it off, he could feel the subtle threat behind Bundy's words. Just then, Gooch reappeared with bottles of 'Ace of Spades' and some champagne glasses. As he began serving the men, Chico started laying out Bundy's options to him.

"Like you've been told, Sosa is gonna share Murdock with you." Chico was under so much pressure, he didn't even notice the look on Yak's face. "Gooch can put you on the security team. That's five hunned a night you can show parole for steady employment. And I've got a lil' something to sweeten the pot." Chico went in his desk drawer and pulled out an envelope. He tossed it to Bundy, and when he checked the contents he had to contain the smile threatening to burst at the corners of his mouth. The envelope contained twenty-thousand dollars. It was almost enough to make Bundy forgive his former crime.

"Oh yeah, that's whassup! As far as the block, I'll take

it. The security gig is a good offer, but I ain't trying to play cop when they done oppressed me for four and change, so here's my counter offer." Bundy knew he was pressing his luck. He just hoped his innuendoes had Chico shook enough to go for his next move. "I'll take the check from the club without the work. Parole don't need to be coming up in your spot checking on me anyway." He turned to Gooch, asking, "Can you make it look like I'm doing independent work, like babysitting a construction site or something."

Gooch shrugged his shoulders, "Whatever the boss says." All eyes went to Chico. Without hesitating, Big Man Bundy looked at Chico with a penetrating stare until he gave in. "Fuck it, if that's what you want."

"It's done then!" Bundy smiled, as Gooch held in his smirk. He wished he could have had something on Chico so he could work some of the soft shoe extortion tactics Bundy was using on the club owner also. He'd seen it done plenty of times in prison, and loved to watch Bundy work it like only a true veteran could.

"One more thing and I need this so badly, that without it, the rest of your good faith ain't worth shit!" Bundy leaned in so Chico could hear him loud and clear. "I need a come up. So I'ma need you to put me on to one of these big willie niggas coming through here. You know home invasion style. But this time I plan on doing it like it's supposed to be done, ya feel me?"

"Bundy, the whole purpose of the club is to provide niggas a way to floss without having to worry 'bout that kind of shit. If word gets out that dudes hanging out here are getting got..."

Bundy cut him short. "It won't! Matter of fact, it'll be so far from the Player's Lounge, they'll never make the connection." Bundy got up and left, before Chico got the impression that he had an option.

Once outside, Yak and Bundy started grinning. They had planned out everything from the dialogue, to the subtle threats. Yak was the first to speak, "That shit went sweet! How'd you know he'd go for it?"

"Yak, this shit is like chess. You've gotta get all your pieces in position for a mate. Chico thinks he's the King, but even so, he only gets to move a square at a time. I'm like a Bishop. See, I don't want to move all across the board like a Queen. I'm a Bishop staying in his lane. But if you peeped the smile Gooch was holding back, then you know that this Bishop just stole a Pawn. If a Bishop steals enough Pawns, it'll eventually tear down a King's first line of defense. And that my nigga, is the first step in check mating your opponent!"

Chapter 5

Respect The Jux.

When Bundy got back to the crib, the sun had already beaten him to the door. For fear of waking Precious, he took off his boots, and tip toed through the living room. By the time he bent down to peek into the bedroom the living room light came on.

"Not even a full twenty-four hours and you're on the same ole' B.S. from back in the day, huh Bryce? Or should I just go on and face the facts and call you Bundy?"

When he looked up, Precious was fully dressed in her work clothes with a frown that said it all. "Another thirty minutes and I would've been forced to call a cab." She was letting Bryce know that his late night habits almost caused her to be late for work. "I didn't stick by you to be going through this shit all over again Bryce. I'm not that young lil' naive girl anymore either. I've got responsibilities now. I've got a career, and can't be showing up late because you like to roam the streets in the one lil' vehicle I've got."

Precious started shaking her head. "Please, don't tell me I've wasted the last four years and three months of my life for nothing. If you have no intentions on doing right by me, then by all means, go!" Precious pointed towards the door to show just how serious she was.

Bundy dropped in front of Precious. He got on his knees, pleading to her, "Babe, don't give up on me just yet. I know I was wrong, but I got a lil' carried away." Bundy placed both hands on Precious' face and kissed her. "I'm gonna go see my P.O., and then I'm going job hunting. Trust me on this, I won't borrow your car without asking, and won't roam the streets 'til dawn."

Precious nodded her head. She wanted to believe Bryce, so she left him at his word. "C'mon, I've gotta get to work." Do you want me to drop you at your Parole Officer's?" As they stepped outside, Precious turned around and saw Yak grinning at her from behind the wheel of his car.

"Yak is gonna drop me off Babe." He could see the disgusted look on his wifey's face.

"So that's who you was running the streets with 'til all types of hours?" Precious remembered Yak from Bundy's arrest; the fact that he'd run straight to his former road dawgs had pissed her off even more.

"Just trust me babe, I'ma do right." He pecked Precious on the cheek before jumping in the ride with Yak. As soon as he got in the whip, Yak had a huge smirk on his face.

"What?" Bundy asked, knowing his crime had jokes.

"Nothing" Yak shrugged, adding, "It ain't that unusual to see the toughest muh'fuckers bitch up when it comes to wifey."

"Fuck you Yak." Bundy laughed, as Yak started to mock Precious and his homie as well.

"See, that's that bullshit Bryce! No pussy fa' Bryce" Yak took his voice down an octave, sounding like Bundy, "Babe please, not pussy punishment. I'm too backed up for that." 'Nah nigga, you wanna fuck wit' Yak and 'em? Let them give you some.' "Babe, you know I ain't going out like that. Yak is a pretty muh'fucker, but he ain't that pretty."

Yak and Bundy started laughing as Precious drove by honking the horn once before heading to work. Bundy nudged Yak. "Knock it off. Take me to parole, and while you wait for me, I want you to get Chico on the horn. This is what I want you to tell him."

"Bryce Johnson. This is my first visit. I came home yesterday."

Have a seat was all that the receptionist said. She didn't even bother to try and hide her disdain for the ex-convicts who came to report to their P.O.'s. Bundy didn't mind because his contempt for authority figures doubled that of the secretary on desk duty.

Bundy glanced around the waiting area. He saw dudes slouched in their chairs wearing iced out crosses, and all different types of expensive watches as well as designer clothes. One man in particular stood out to Bundy. He looked to be about the same age as him, but sat in the parole office sporting a three piece suit. Bundy noticed that the man must have had an occupation where such a wardrobe was a necessity, noting it wasn't the type of outfit a person put together because he had to. This suit was tailored to perfection. It was a black Armani which he coordinated with a charcoal gray patterned tie, tied in a Windsor knot and a handkerchief stuffed in his left breast pocket. A briefcase sat tucked between his legs.

Bundy made eye contact with the man, who gave him a half smile before nodding in his direction. For some reason the man looked familiar to Bundy. As soon as the well dressed man's P.O. entered, he wasted no time skipping the other goons in the room for the tailored gentleman. A minute later, another P.O. came to the door. This time it was a woman.

"Mr. Johnson?" The female calling Bundy's name had her hand on the doorknob, while leaning halfway into the waiting area. Bundy got up and followed the woman into her back office. When he entered the office, he noticed the array of African statues, and other Afro centric paraphernalia. The sight of them led Bundy to believe he'd been assigned a pushover as a P.O.

She didn't say a word for the first five minutes. She just sat in her chair going over Bundy's file. Being that it was based on his criminal history, there wasn't much for her to go through. She couldn't quite put her finger on it, but there was something about Bundy's instant offense, coupled with his demeanor that had his P.O.'s gut telling her there was more to the man before her than the paperwork revealed. When she looked up, she finally spoke.

"Mr. Johnson, my name is Ms. Williams. I'll more than likely be your Parole Officer until you violate or max-out. I won't stand for the nonsense, and I am going to be on you until you prove I don't have to be." Ms. Williams reached into the drawer of her desk and pulled out a cup and a plastic bag. "Can you supply me with a clean urine sample?" Bundy nodded. "Is that a yes, because I don't do sign language."

"Yes" Bundy mumbled.

"Very well put. I have a lot of men that come in here trying to explain to me that they'd gotten high while incarcerated. All that would have gotten you was in a program Mr. Johnson." She pointed the cup at Bundy while she spoke. "As you can see, I'm hard on my parolees, reason being, there are too many struggling single mothers out here busting their asses because of men like you Mr. Johnson."

Ms. Williams got up and Bundy followed her to the back of the office area, to a small bathroom reserved for urine sample testing. During their short walk, Bundy was distracted by Ms. Williams' phat ass shaking to and fro', and didn't realize she was going to test him personally until they were at the bathroom door. Bundy knew that the normal protocol was for her to get a male P.O. to do the deed. He figured there must have been a touch of freakiness behind her no-nonsense demeanor. Bundy concentrated on her ass, imagining him hitting it from the back, which caused him to get a slight erection.

If you wanna see some sausage, I'm gonna beef up for you bitch, Bundy thought, grinning all the while.

"Here you go Mr. Johnson. Don't be shy." As Bundy pulled out, Ms. Williams turned her head in the opposite direction. Bundy was finding it hard to relieve himself as his penis started growing, but he refused to deny himself the pleasure of flashing his oppressor. He looked towards the wall, hoping that this would prompt Ms. Williams to sneak a peek at his manhood. Sure enough, she took the bait.

"Mmm," he heard her mumble, not knowing her thoughts were hardly what he would have wanted to hear. After relieving himself, Bundy shook his dick, over exaggerating the need, as she handed him the bag to put the cup inside.

"Back to my office Mr. Johnson," she said, but thought, *Freak ass nigga. I'll ride that big motherfucker, take your cash, then lock your horny lil' ass up without missing a wink of sleep!* When they got back to her office, Ms. Williams handed Bundy a sheet of paper.

"I want you to fill out this sheet every time you go job hunting. I will give you a month to find a job, but after that, if you don't find one, I will find one for you. And trust me; you won't like the labor or the pay if I have to find the job for you." She waved him out of her office. "I'll be expecting to hear from you two weeks from today Mr. Johnson."

Bundy got into the elevator and just before it closed, the suited ex-con boarded the elevator behind him. The man was all smiles as he entered. Bundy did a double take at the man, who was still cheesing at him.

"I know you?" Bundy asked, back in beast mode.

"Bryce Johnson a.k.a Bundy. Nigga, you don't remember me?"

Bundy squinted, but it was the voice that jogged his memory loose. "Joseph?" Then it came to him. "Oh shit, Money. Joseph Thomas! Yo, I ain't even recognize yo' ass in them threads baby boy." Bundy bear hugged his old road dawg. "What the deal, yo?" He finally released Joseph.

"Chilling my nigga. Just maintaining."

"Whatchu doing?" Bundy felt the fabric of his lapel.

"Same shit! Don't let the vines fool you, that's just a tactic I use to keep my P.O. at bay. A suit works wonders for the image, ya' know? The same broad that'll grip her purse when you walk by, will nod in greeting if you're in a suit."

"So where you heading now?"

"To change into my street clothes so I can get back to my business. I got a few spots, and I'm trying to expand. I got this lil' Italian broad, hooked me up; plugged me into some heavy hitters Uptown."

"I heard in the pen you was doing it up."

"No doubt, but listen." Money leaned into Bundy, looking around before whispering, "We don't wanna get caught in here pollying, so take my number and holler at me later." Just that quick, Money was gone. Bundy made a mental note to cop himself a suit before his next reporting date.

When Bundy hit the pavement, Yak was across the street chatting with two cuties that seemed to be engrossed in whatever lines he was feeding them. "I'm not a pimp baby girl, I'm an opportunist. As an opportunist, there is no way in the world I'm just gonna let ya'll fine asses strut pass ole' Yak without me trying to holler. I like the finest things in life and that includes my women, so I'm happy to announce that you girls qualify." The girls started giggling, and Yak knew he was one line away from sealing the deal. Just then, Bundy tapped on the window, cutting short Yak's spiel.

"You ready?" In an instant, Yak was all business. He turned the ignition, as Bundy jumped in, pulling off without so much as a goodbye. By the time Yak made the right turn on Hillside Avenue, he was updating Bundy on his conversation with Chico.

"I don't know how you do what you do, but Chico had no problem wit' it like you said."

"It's just like I told you Yak." Bundy started counting off his logic. "Basically, I'm working two angles here. First, I keep Chico comfortable by coming to him with every lil' problem I got. From his perspective, I wouldn't solicit his help if I had animosity towards him, so his mind is somewhat at ease. Trust me, he's still leery of me, he's just got a good poker face. He figures my pride wouldn't ask him for help if I felt a way about that sucker shit he did. Second, I get to keep the pressure on him. I'm bringing up my needs any and every chance I get. I don't care if that nigga Chico brings up the weather. I'ma be like, Yeah, it's hot out, but have you got that dude lined up for me to jux, yet?"

Both men laughed. When they neared 183rd, sure enough, Chico was right where he'd been instructed to be. Yak pulled into the space in front of them, and that's when Gooch stepped out of the car and went over to Chico's side.

This fool don't trust me just yet, Bundy thought. At the moment, he didn't expect anything less. "What's good?" Bundy bumped fists, not wanting to overplay his hand.

Chico followed suit. "Ain't shit! I'm in a rush, so here." He handed Bundy a set of car keys which he quickly placed in his pocket.

Bundy had Yak explain to Chico what had transpired between him and Precious. Yak told Chico that Bundy planned on purchasing a vehicle, but needed to borrow a loaner until the paperwork was done.

"I parked the joint around the corner. You know how these crackers be, son. They'll assume some funny style shit is going down. Next thing you know, they'll have us all hemmed up, thinking they done found 'em a drug bust or something. I can't afford that."

Bundy jumped in. "Good looking!" then leaned in, whispering, "What's up wit' that other thing we talked about?" You find me one of those big ballers at the club yet? A nigga gotta eat Chico."

"I'm still working on it." The subject caused Chico to give Bundy the bum's rush. He threw his thumb and pinky to his ear, mouthing the words "call me," as he got in his Audi with Gooch and pulled off.

As soon as they walked around the corner, Bundy pulled out the set of keys and hit the alarm. When the car alarm chirped, Bundy had to hit it again to make sure his mind wasn't playing tricks on him. Again, the car chirped. Bundy looked at Yak, who had a huge grin on his face.

"Daaamn! Chico must really be sorry Big Man!" The source of their surprise was a platinum gray Aston Martin DB9 with Asanti AF-b 139's. The rims were twenty-two inches with what appeared to be hardly enough rubber to make a slow turn without the chrome touching concrete. "It ain't the car that shocks me but the fact that he'd lend such a beauty to yo' brutish ass!" Both men laughed.

Yak didn't think twice about leaving his whip where it was parked to enjoy the ride the Aston Martin had to offer. When Bundy hit the ignition, Jay-Z's 'All I Need' started blasting through the speakers.

"Fuck it! I guess I got my swagger back. Mamma they said I killed a man, but I guess I got the dagger back." Bundy started remixing his own lyrics to Jigga's classic,

"It's the Rock! We back in the heezy. The one on Farmers and one-oh-nineezah!"

"So, where to?" Yak asked.

"I'm finna hit one of these Hillside car lots and cop me a whip."

Yak shook his head. "Nah, go to Queens Blvd. I wanna show you something."

"Can't it wait? I want these wheels."

"Trust me, we on the same page."

"Fuck it, Queens Boulevard it is."

"Precious, have you heard a word I've said?" At the sound of her name, Precious snapped out of her trance.

"Huh? Oh, I'm sorry Loretta. I was just daydreaming." Precious knew how Loretta felt about her relationship with Bryce, so she was reluctant to share her feelings with her girlfriend. Just knowing Bryce had been in prison was enough for Loretta to label him trouble, and Precious wasn't in the mood for 'I told you so's.'

"You wanna talk about it?" Loretta asked, taking a seat at Precious' desk. Precious shook her head. "C'mon now. It's obvious that something's on your mind. They say it helps when you vent to a friend."

It took a few minutes, but Precious finally let out a deep breath, giving in. "It's Bryce already." Loretta nodded her head as if she knew the rest of the story. "He's already running the streets Loretta. It hasn't even been a full twenty-four hours and he comes home at dawn, without so much as an explanation. He borrowed my car without asking, and at first I thought it was stolen. He didn't even bother to think that had I reported it stolen, he could have gotten pulled over, and the police contact alone could have sent him back up on a violation."

Loretta grabbed Precious' hand, reasoning, "Lucky for him, one of you were doing some rational thinking."

"You know what scares me Loretta? It's the fact that he's so blinded by material things. He wants the success without putting in the work."

"Precious, hon, that's not even success. The route he wants is reserved for gangsters. I don't know if it's the rap videos that got our men thinking their masculinity is defined by the price of their ride or what. They need to grow up and realize that half of those rappers they try to emulate don't even live the life they portray in those videos."

"I try and tell him that, but he argues that even most

of his boys have got it like that. I know it is a very small percentage that may be in a good position in life. The rest are struggling like the rest of us to make ends meet. The other few are just immature enough to pull that Mercedes up to their Momma's house where they stay in the basement for $400 a month." Loretta's laugh caused Precious to cheer up.

"I know that's right Precious! I've been caught out there a couple of times at the club myself. Now a red flag goes up if a dude tries to tell me he wants to chill at the hotel because he doesn't like people knowing where he lives." This time, both women started laughing. Then Loretta got serious. "I know you think I'm gonna hit you with, I told you so, but the truth is you've waited almost a half decade for this man Precious, so I honestly think there's no need to make any rash decisions or ultimatums. Give Bryce time. Hopefully he'll figure out what he wants out of life."

"I hope so. I want a simple life Loretta. But he measures his happiness and self worth through possessions and that is not what God has intended for us."

Loretta interrupted. "Give it time hon, you feel like taking an early lunch? My treat," Loretta waved her paycheck in the air, letting Precious know it was a one time offer.

Precious laughed, "I might be a lil' stressed out, but I'm no fool. C'mon before you find a cute pair of pumps on sale and change your mind."

"Yeah, that might be a good idea." They both laughed, making their way to a restaurant across the street from their work office.

Yak took one last look at the business card before telling Bundy "Make a left, that's the lot right there." They pulled into the lot, and the owner immediately took notice of the platinum Aston Martin. As Bundy got out and stretched he asked Yak, "So, what's so important 'bout this particular dealership?"

"You'll see," Yak stated, steady grinning. All of a sudden, a piercing scream came from the trailer at the rear of car lot.

"My muh'fucking baby Bundy! When they let you out?" Tina jumped right into Bundy's arms before he could stop her.

"Oh shit, Tina?" He put her down and faced her at arms length.

Tina spun around, letting Bundy get a good look at what the last four years and three months had deprived him of. "Last time I saw you was right before you caught your bid, and you haven't changed a bit." Tina squeezed his bicep and bit her bottom lip, as she made a slight hissing noise.

"You miss me, Big Man?" Yak started laughing.

"No doubt! You working here, or milking the owner?"

Tina tapped him playfully on the arm. "I'm working, and not like you think," she said winking.

It was Tina's house that Bundy and Yak had gone to before the requested liquor run that had gotten Bundy knocked. Tina was his chick on the side. All her friends were hustlers whose skills ranged from boosting, transporting, fake driver's licenses and credit card scams. If there was an angle for money to be made, Tina more than likely had a home girl who could assist in making it happen. So Bundy knew Yak had brought him to the lot she worked at for a reason. Bundy planned on getting up with Tina at a later date, and after telling her so, got right down to the business at hand.

"So Tina, what's the deal with an employee discount?" Bundy was kicking the tires on a Lexus LS.

"Oh, you looking to cop something? Matter of fact,

when did them crackers let yo' ass out, and why you ain't been by to see me?" Tina had her hands on her hips, adding, "And don't try beating me in the head 'cause you know my address ain't change nigga."

"Chill ma, damn! A nigga just touched the bricks yesterday." Bundy was making his way towards the rear of the lot where the less expensive cars were stationed.

"Is that you Bundy?" Tina nodded towards the Aston Martin, "cause if so, you in the wrong part of the lot. That baby will pretty much get you anything you like on this lot."

"Nah, I borrowed that from one of my mans." Bundy caught himself. "I mean one of my associates."

"Shoot, I'm gonna have to plug your associate into one of my girls if he got shit like that to be lending a nigga. I can't imagine what he got his bitch pushing!" Tina bit her bottom lip, adding; "So whatchu trying to do Bundy, trade in, finance, or purchase it straight up?"

"I guess I'm trying to purchase it."

"You holding like that, huh?"

Bundy could tell Tina was mentally trying to assess his net worth. It caused him to start chuckling. "You're bugged out Tee. Haven't changed a bit."

"What? I'm just asking. It's my job to ask." They both

started to laugh.

Yak was in the corner checking out a pearl white 760 BMW. Bundy called Yak over, and nodded towards a cherry red Dodge Magnum. Yak shrugged his shoulders. "Don't ask me. After the Aston, it's hard to pay attention to any of the whips in this joint."

Bundy turned to Tina. "I'm looking for something inconspicuous."

"Check you out! In-con-spic-u-ous. Lemme find out you want a creep mobile. You boys back on ya'll grizzly, huh? You ain't wasting no time playboy." Bundy's grin pretty much answered her question. As Tina walked them over to an all black Dodge Charger, she hit Bundy with the facts that she knew would interest him most. "It belonged to some hustling cat out in Jersey City. I think he used it for transporting, 'cause he never bothered to wash it, but kept it in mint condition. He kept the stock rims on it and the tint is perfect. Its light enough not to get pulled over, yet the black interior allows the occupants a decent degree of shade." Tina reached in and popped the hood. "And it's a Hemi!"

When Bundy checked, it was just as Tina said. The car was in mint condition. He liked it because it wasn't the type of vehicle that would cause a vic to look twice. "How much?"

"They want 14 grand, but they're willing to take 12. I suggest you put about 8 on it, so you don't alert the authorities that you're spending over ten thou. Besides, you need to start rebuilding your credit since yo' shit been inactive so long." By then, Tina, Bundy, and Yak had entered the trailer so that Tina could check Bundy's credit file on the computer. "You should have had Precious get some joint credit cards and a joint account so your credit report could show some type of activity. Don't sweat it though, ain't no way my boss is turning down a sixty percent down payment. I don't care if he gotta co-sign the loan himself."

As Tina laughed Bundy shook his head. "I just can't get over the fact somebody gave your larcenous ass access to peoples credit history."

Tina nudged him on the arm. "Sshh! Nigga, you trying to blow me up?" Bundy could see she was dead ass serious.

Player's Lounge

"May I help you, Sir?" The waitress had just dropped off another two bottles of 'Ace of Spades.' She was the only one brave enough to deal with the arrogant customer. In reality, she wasn't as courageous as her coworkers thought. The man just so happened to be a big spender, and she could use the generous tips.

"If you wanna help me out, pretend you dropped something so I can measure the spread on that ass of yours. If you're lucky, I might allow you to help me get my nuts out the sand." "Psst!" The barmaid spun on her heels. No amount of money was worth her dignity.

The arrogant patron was a dealer from Corona, Queens named Fernando Morales. Fernando grew up on Macintosh Avenue, and had a small army of Latin Kings at his disposal. Fernando was short tempered and narcissistic. He got put on to the drug game through his uncle, Felipe, who passed on the family business due to what he termed a 'forced retirement.' Actually, it was just a fancy way to refer to the 20 year federal prison sentence he had. Fernando was loud, obnoxious, and extremely flashy. He was also soft as tapioca pudding. Needless to say, he came with all the bad habits that stemmed from newly acquired money.

"What? What'd I do? Did I say something wrong?" He asked his posse. The question was rhetorical. Fernando had a crew of yes men who agreed to anything he said.

"No Papi. She should be honored if you allowed her the privilege of swallowing your kids." The woman doing the talking was his Spanish Mami Melina. She took the cashmere trench off of Fernando's shoulders while one of his henchmen pulled out his chair for him.

Fernando kissed Melina on her forehead. "That's why I love you Mami. You always know the right thing to say."

Meanwhile, downstairs, in front of Chico's office, the waitresses of the Player's Lounge were giving Gooch an earful. "Uh-uh, I refuse! You can fire me now, but make it official, 'cause I'm gonna need the paperwork in order to receive unemployment," a waitress named Catalina protested.

"I don't see the problem Goochi." The hostess Catalina always added an 'i' to Gooch's handle. "Tell Chico to throw his ass out!"

"Chico's upstairs talking to Fernando now. He's new money. Dudes like him finally touch some paper and it tends to go to their head. Right now, he's giving the world his ass to kiss. Kicking him out of the club may start problems that aren't conducive to the business we're trying to run."

"Well I hope Chico has an apron and uniform, 'cause I'm not serving him." The rest of the girls voiced their agreement out loud. Gooch sighed. Every time Fernando visited the Lounge it was the same problems.

Back in the main lounge, Chico was trying to reason with Fernando. His ego plus the presence of his entourage, made it damn near impossible to talk to him. Fernando was in full stunt mode. "I understand you fully Chico. Good help is hard to find." Fernando spread his arms like a comedian who'd just delivered a punch line, and right on cue, his yes men started laughing. He continued on. "But if you want, I'm willing to invest a few chicas and pesos into turning your lil' rib shack into something special. Shit, I'll even buy out Deuce." Fernando was in rare form, and didn't plan on giving Chico a way out. "Even better, how 'bout we turn his mixtapes on to Salsa and Reggaeton? That way, the Latino's will know you haven't forgotten your heritage."

Chico was fuming. He placed the bottles of 'Ace of Spades' on the table and tried his best to step away from Fernando without wearing his emotions on his sleeve. Halfway down the stairs, Gooch grabbed Chico by the arm.

"People are breaking out Chico. That muh'fucker's not only arrogant, he's straight up rude! Lemme go out there wit' the boys and tighten him up?" Chico was shaking his head. He knew not to cause a scene. Besides, he didn't need Fernando trying to retaliate at his place of business.

That's when it came to him. His face lit up so bright, Gooch had to inquire as to the source of his change in mood. "What? Talk to me."

"Gooch, lemme ask you something. Out of all that hot air Fernando be blowing, do you think he's the type to bang it out, or respect the jux?"

Gooch began grinning as he caught onto what Chico was implying. "C'mon Chico, that dude ain't never experienced no front line action. He'd definitely respect the jux. Probably would fold like a bad hand too. Why, what you got planned?"

"Might as well kill two birds with one stone, huh?" A few seconds passed before Chico spoke his next words. "Gooch, get Bundy on the phone. I think we found him his come up."

Chapter 6
The Come - Up!

Four days later...

"What the fuck is taking this fool so long?" Yak complained. Bundy polished off the last chicken breast they were eating. He tossed it back in the bucket, and then chucked the KFC bucket in the rear seat of the Dodge Charger.

The newly acquired ride was a mess. A blanket laid in the back seat from Bundy's last three days of surveillance. Unlike Yak, Bundy didn't care how long it took for Fernando to find his way home. Knowing where he laid his head was ninety percent of the task. He knew that Fernando was going to be coming from the Player's Lounge. He and Yak waited to catch him slipping so that they could collect every dime he had stashed in his house.

An hour passed, and finally Fernando pulled into the driveway with Melina two steps behind him. "Showtime!" Bundy nudged Yak out of his sleep, putting on his black leather gloves, while mumbling instructions to Yak.

"Don't forget. Stick and move! We're in and out like a robbery is supposed to be. And toss the guns!" They waited for another two hours, and Bundy's patience was killing Yak. Finally, he hit the driver's side door.

They went to the rear of the house. Yak reached into his bag of tools, and retrieved a miniature crowbar. They had previously checked the perimeter of the house, and agreed that the backdoor was indeed the structure's weak point. Yak stuck the crowbar into the wedge of the door lock, prying it apart with ease. The two of them crept through the house with their guns cocked and aimed at any opposition they might encounter. After a few minutes, they realized the house was empty with the exception of Fernando and Melina. That's when Bundy heard the moans escaping the couple's bedroom door. They slid up the stairs until they were right outside the door, and that's when they heard Fernando's voice.

"This is your threesome bitch, one in the ass and one in that tight lil' baby box. Which dick is bigger, huh?"

When Bundy put his ear to the door he could hear the sound of flesh smacking against flesh.

"Oh Daddy! Your dick is the biggest!" Melina squealed, as she got pounded from the rear. Bundy expected to run up on three people, so he held up three fingers to Yak and kicked in the door. When they entered the room they stood face to face with Fernando and Melina. Bundy looked at Fernando's butt naked form and realized the third person in their ménage was a strap on dildo underneath Fernando's own penis.

"Look at this freak ass nigga Bo!" Yak was still straightening out his ski mask. "Fernando, why is you trying to compete with a dildo anyway homie?" Yak started to snicker, until Fernando got fly out the mouth.

"If you know who I am, I'm surprised you were still foolish enough to break into my house. You boys must have a death wish."

Bundy and Yak looked at each other, then back to Fernando. Bundy was the one to speak first. "You're as arrogant as I've been told Fernando. That's gonna make this even easier." Bundy gave Yak the nod, causing him to leap into action. He forced Fernando and Melina into the bedroom chairs, and duct taped them to it.

Yak disappeared for a few seconds and came back with a bucket of water that he placed underneath Melina's bare feet. He then went into his duffle bag and pulled out a taser gun. "Now we get to see just how much you love this broad of yours. I put her feet in the bucket of water to intensify the taser shock. So answer my friend's questions very carefully, or your bitch is gonna be in a lot of pain."

Bundy took his cue by stepping in close to Fernando's ear, whispering, "Where's it at Fernando, the drugs, the cash, and the jewels?"

"I keep it in a stash house across town. The place is surrounded by mi sold..." Bundy smacked him across the mouth with the barrel of his Desert Eagle.

"You've got one more time to lie amigo, and zap! The bitch gets it." Yak was playing with the taser in Melina's face.

"I swear to you. If I was going to..." Before Fernando could finish, Yak had hit Melina with the first shock. Her scream should have been enough to soften Fernando's resolve, but he stuck to his guns. Fernando realized that the taser was no ordinary one. Melina's flesh was practically smoldering. Fernando could smell the lingering odor of burnt flesh. Melina drifted in and out of consciousness. He knew the mark on her right breast would leave a permanent scar.

Bundy gave Fernando a minute to digest what was happening. He studied Fernando and saw that the sight of Melina half conscious did nothing to him. Yak moved the taser to her other breast, as Melina's eyes got wide with fear.

"Nigga, I ain't gonna lie, I didn't think you had it in you to stand any torture, but since you so gangster we gon' play this thing out to the end." Yak tasered Melina for a second time, and instantly, she fell out. Had Yak known Melina's story, he would have known that Fernando's heart came from the fact that he didn't give a damn about her being tortured. As she drifted out of consciousness, her mind went back to her original meeting with Fernando.

Melina was the only offspring of Jorge and Jacinda Torres. Two immigrants who migrated from the Dominican Republic and illegally made their way into the U.S. Jorge and Jacinda worked for Felipe as lawns man and housekeeper respectively. Jorge needed money to get his older sister into the States. Seeing the many antiques that Felipe owned, he talked his wife Jacinda into stealing a rare statue in hopes of selling it to get his sister safe passage. When the theft was discovered, Jorge had no idea of the lengths Felipe would undergo to unearth the perpetrator. Through torture, Jacinda finally broke, and not only did Felipe make Jacinda his sex slave in exchange for her life, but he took Jorge's life as payment. Melina was too young for Felipe. He made her a servant until she reached her teens, then turned her over to Fernando to do as he pleased. Since then, she'd been his servant in every way imaginable.

"Wake the fuck up, bitch!" Yak smacked flames out of Melina. A few seconds later, she came to.

Bundy sighed. "I don't have time for all this torture shit Fernando. Where's the loot?" Bundy pressed the barrel of the .50 caliber Desert Eagle against Melina's temple. Her eyes became mere slits, as she gave Fernando a look that could kill. Yak peeped it, and that gave him an idea.

"Hold up!" Yak walked over to Fernando, taunting him. "You think you tough, huh?" Yak cocked back his fist, Smack! The force of his punch snapped Fernando's head back violently. He put the taser to Fernando's neck, as he growled, "I wanna see how tough this muh'fucker really is." But before Yak could zap him, he started copping a plea.

"No! Wait! I...The safe is in the basement behind the dryer. The combination is 24 left, 66 right 87 left."

Before Yak could turn to Bundy for approval, the big man was already on his way to the basement. Yak looked at Melina, and saw she must have been thinking the same thing that he was. After a few seconds, Yak voiced his thoughts aloud. "You's a bitch! Here it is your broad's got more balls than her man. At least she took a couple of shocks." He turned to Melina, adding, "My bad ma. I thought this nigga might have more love for you than himself. Come to find out, he ain't give two fucks about yo' ass. Had I known Fernando only cared about himself, I could've saved myself a lotta time, and you a lotta pain."

This gave Yak another idea. He whispered in Melina's ear, "I'm gonna put this gun to your head, make you put that strap-on tight and fuck that clown. This is your chance to get even while it looks like you were forced to do it. If you think you can't do it, just remember this, he was going to let us do you any kind of way."

Meanwhile, in the basement, Bundy hefted the dryer to the side, and sure enough Fernando had a huge wall safe hidden right where he said it would be.

"24 left, 66 right, and 87 left," he mumbled. He closed

his eyes as he spun the handle. "Cha-ching!" The safe popped open and he loaded what looked to be at least a quarter-million in cash, and three kilos of cocaine.

Yak could hear Bundy running up the stairs. Thinking that Fernando had lied to his crimee, Yak knew the Corona kingpin was in for a beat down. Yak grinned to himself, knowing whatever Bundy had planned would pale in comparison to what he was currently going through.

"I got it. You check for any valuables?" Yak held up a handful of jewelry. Then it came to Bundy. "Why you out here? Don't tell me you killed 'em?" Yak smiled. Bundy could hear the muffled sounds coming from the bedroom.

"Nigga, what is you..." as he went to open the door, Bundy was met by a stomach turning sight. Fernando was handcuffed to the bedposts and blindfolded. There was a wet urine stain underneath him from where Melina had urinated on his head. The sight that had nauseated Bundy the most was Melina plowing into Fernando's rear with the dildo he had used on her earlier. "You done lost your muh'fucking mind! What made you do some perverted shit like that?"

Yak shrugged his shoulders. "I figured the broad deserved to get the nigga back." He started grinning like a Cheshire cat.

"Let's be out, I ain't trying to see that shit." Bundy made his way down the steps with Yak in tow. Yak started laughing for no reason.

"What the fuck is wrong witchu?" Bundy asked as they got in the car. Yak's laughter was becoming contagious.

"Nah, I was just thinking," Bundy was waiting to hear the rest, "it smelled like that nigga Fernando shitted on himself." Bundy just shook his head as the two of them made their way back to Murdock Ave.

"Precious, where you at babe?" Bundy came into the crib more optimistic than Precious had seen him since his release. Little did she know, the source of his newfound outlook was $130,000 in cold hard cash, and a kilo and a half of pure Columbian cocaine. The best part of it all was the fact that the proceeds were only Bundy's half of the jux. Yak had an equal share of the take stashed where only he could get to it. Bundy had a brand new Ralph Lauren Purple Label suit slung over his arm.

"Precious?" He called out a second time. Precious came out of the kitchen in an off white slip with slippers on. "I'm right here Bryce. You're going to wake the neighbors with all that yelling and carrying on."

Bundy slipped into her arms, kissing her softly, as he announced their plans for the night. "We're going out tonight." He handed her some cash, further explaining, "The Player's Lounge is having some sort of shindig, and we've been invited by Chico to attend. Yak is bringing Candy, so take that dough and buy you some threads. I gotta go check something out. I'll be back." He kissed her on the cheek, and was once again out the door. When Precious looked at the money he handed her, she saw what appeared to be at least fifteen grand.

When Bundy reached Murdock, Yak had a glow that only a three kilo come up could produce. Yak wasted no time in breaking down his first brick for distribution. He'd also put out the word that he was now in the business of selling weight. Since the work didn't cost him a dime, Yak sold his product for less than anyone around the way.

Bundy didn't care too much for hustling drugs, so he gave Yak his brick and a half to do the same. When the Charger pulled up to the corner, Yak jumped in. He had a fat blunt between his lips.

"Where the fuck you been Yak? I been calling your cell all morning, and I get pushed straight to voice mail. Lemme find out! It ain't even a whole day, and you already showing your niggas yo' ass cause you done came up." Bundy joked. He and Yak were in high spirits, so Yak started feeding into the jokes.

"Time is money B, and I ain't got time to be fucking wit' you penny ante dudes." Yak brushed his shoulder off, then got serious. "On the real, my phone's been ringing off the hook since we put the word out on this work. Niggas is loving it! I been lying to Money and 'em that there's more where it came from." As an afterthought he added, "I'm gonna have to find a good connect though." Bundy knew Yak was done with the robberies. To him, it was just the means to an end. His plan was to use Bundy as a way to keep Sosa at bay, and feed him until they slowly edged him out of the picture. After a minute of small talk, Bundy changed the subject.

"We going to the Player's Lounge tonight. Bring Candy, 'cause I'm bringing Precious. Chico's bringing his lady too. He said we 'posed to be celebrating my release, but I think he's throwing in the celebration of putting Fernando's ass out of the Lounge's spotlight."

"Word! I know he ain't trying to show his face in public for a minute. I know I wouldn't. Matter of fact, niggas would'a had to kill me 'fore I go for that shit Fernando went through."

Bundy laughed, as he told Yak, "I went by the Lounge, and the nigga Chico tells me that whatever we got from the jux is ours. I'm glad he said that, 'cause I wasn't planning on giving him shit!" Yak nodded in agreement.

"What time is this get together?"

"Around ten tonight."

"I'll see you at ten then." Yak stepped out of the car, adding, "Candy will be glad to hear it. She hasn't seen Precious in a while."

"Where's she at anyway?" Bundy asked.

"Out shopping, you know how the ladies do." Yak gave Bundy dap, as he skirted his Charger back towards Union Turnpike.

"Precious, you ready?" Bundy had just awakened from a nap, gotten dressed, and was now waiting on Precious to make her way down the stairs. It was 9:45 pm, leaving them fifteen minutes to hit the highway and get to the Player's Lounge. Bundy knew they were going to be late.

"I'm coming!" Precious strutted down the steps in an off white sequined gown by Roberto Cavalli, with matching pumps. As beautiful as she looked, all Bundy could concentrate on was the fact that Precious didn't buy anything new.

"Why you ain't go shopping?"

"What, you don't like the outfit?"

"Nah, I'm just saying, I wanted you to treat yourself to something nice. You look fine babe." *Bundy made a mental note for the future to purchase Precious something anytime he splurged on himself.* Tonight was about him and Yak coming up in the game, and he wanted Precious to represent his come up via designer labels from head to toe. "Let's be out."

It took them thirty minutes to arrive at the Player's Lounge. The lot in front of the club was laced with every whip from BMWs to Ferraris. Yak had recently copped a milk white 760 Beemer, and Chico's Aston Martin sat in the reserved parking area. He even caught a glimpse of an all black Rolls Royce Phantom that caused him to park his Dodge Charger towards the rear of the lot. *All the while, he was thinking to himself to go to Queens Boulevard, so that he could cash in on the trade-in Tina had suggested to him earlier.*

As soon as they entered the club, Bundy saw Chico waving him and Precious over. "What took you so long?" Chico asked, embracing his homie.

"You know how the women are." Bundy didn't get a chance to get the rest out, as Precious quickly defended herself. "If you want the proper results, you have to have the patience for perfection." This caused everyone at the table to laugh.

"Precious. Long time no see girl. Give your big bro' some love." As Precious hugged Chico, Bundy came in right on cue.

"Out of trust for my baby, I'll let that big bro' thing ride, but you ain't got too many show me some loves left." Chico grinned, because for a moment, it felt like old times again.

"Girl, I know Chico ain't the only one you see here." Candy waved Precious towards her. "Gimme some!" They kissed each other on the cheek, and Candy wiped the traces of her lipstick off Precious' face.

"You're looking good Candy."

"Thanks. You like?" Candy spun around for Precious, showing off her new outfit. "I bought it today." She showed off the Dries Van Noten dress and stuck out her Alexander McQueen wooden platform sandals so Precious could get a good look.

Bundy was more into the labels than Precious, so the $2500 dollar Nancy Gonzalez purse on the table didn't escape him. Although Chico's woman Sabrina was the most conservative as far as outfits went, Bundy chalked it up to the fact that everyone knew Chico was balling, so she felt she had nothing to prove. Truth be told, Sabrina had the same outlook on material possessions as Precious. Candy was the one who was as bad as Yak and Bundy when it came to getting fly.

"Is that Roberto Cavalli?"

"Yeah, I just dug it out the closet. All of this was so sudden, but you know I keep a lil' something in case of an emergency dinner date." Precious teased.

"Well, you can't go wrong with Roberto." Candy drew the name out as if the man was a God, adding, "A classic by any other name is still a classic."

Precious humbly acknowledged the compliment. Bundy took it as Candy just trying to be nice. He wished for the umpteenth time that Precious would have gone shopping. He was too into himself to notice everyone else at the table had thought nothing of it and had already moved on to another subject.

"When you get a chance, Gooch has your paycheck. I figured you'd want to get that to your P.O. as soon as possible, ya' know?"

"No doubt!" Bundy grinned. A waitress came over and

took their order while Yak excused himself from the table. "Excuse me ladies, I've gotta make a trip to the men's room." Yak had to hike up his jeans in order to secure the two Ruger P90's in the small of his back. Candy watched with pride as her man bopped towards the bathroom in a black cashmere blazer with a white button up, Omavi jeans, and a pair of hard bottom black Mauri gators. Bundy had on the same outfit, but opted for a gray suit jacket with matching gators. Chico, as the owner of the club, kept it classy as always in an all black suit, with a black V-neck sweater.

Inside the bathroom, Yak takes a leak, and then adjusts his guns as Gooch enters. Gooch takes a minute to look himself over in the mirror, and Yak is pretty sure the bouncer is stalling for time. Yak's suspicions are confirmed when he makes his way to the sink to wash his hands.

"You're packing a lotta hardware for a simple couple's night out, Yak." "Old habits die hard Gooch."

Gooch had been around a lot of gangsters in his forty years on earth. He was also a good judge of character, so he felt he possessed the ability to distinguish the real from the fake. As far as he was concerned, Yak and Bundy were the real thing.

"What's on your mind Gooch?" Yak got straight to the

point. He was looking in the mirror, while adjusting the platinum chains on his neck.

"I was there when Chico finally gave in to the decision to call ya'll about Fernando. I been wanting to get some of the clowns that come through here stuntin'. I've had my eye on a certain cat that frequents the spot, but if Chico found out he'd have a fit. I figured we could keep this one between us, and maybe you'd get Bundy to hear me out, so I could get in where I fit in?"

Yak nodded his understanding. Although he was more of a hustler than a stickup kid, the possibilities of a second easy score appealed to him. "Isn't Bundy 'posed to see you 'bout a paycheck or sum'thin'?"

Gooch whipped out the check, grinning, "Got it right here."

"Wait here. I'm gonna send him down."

When Yak got upstairs, the ladies were chatting away, but Yak felt a tension in Chico he hadn't sensed earlier. Before he could catch on to the source of Chico's discomfort, Bundy nodded his head in the direction of a table to the far left of the lounge. To Yak's surprise, he saw Fernando in full stunt mode, causing his usual set of theatrics. Yak gave a subtle nod, letting Bundy know he'd be on point in the event Fernando had figured out their identities.

"I bumped into Gooch downstairs. He said your paycheck is burning a hole in his pocket."

"I'll get it later."

"Nah B, you should get it now." Bundy and Yak had too many years together for the big man not to catch the underlying message in Yak's statement. He politely excused himself from the table and went downstairs to seek out Gooch. As Bundy left, Yak noticed that Melina was no longer a part of Fernando's entourage.

By the time Bundy made it down the first flight of steps, Gooch was waiting to escort him into Chico's office. The first thing he did was hand Bundy his check. "That should keep your P.O. off your ass for a minute."

"That's what's up." Bundy tucked the check in his inside breast pocket. "So, what is it that you had to tell me?"

Gooch leaned in as if Chico's office was wiretapped. "I was telling Yak how, I admired the way you handled Chico. I've been trying to get him to let me get a few of these dudes for the longest. I guess he couldn't brush you off like he did me. Anyway, I got a jux lined up, and if you'll let me ride, we all stand to make a decent dollar off of this cat. What you say?"

"I'll tell you what. Meet me on Murdock, near the rock where LL did his video back in the days. You know where that's at?" Gooch knew exactly where Bundy was talking about.

"Farmers and 109. I got family over there." Before they could conclude their business, a knock on the door took both men out of their zone.

"Goochie, they need you upstairs. Fernando is back on his mess."

Both men rushed upstairs. Bundy was more concerned that Yak would cause a major scene. He didn't want Precious to witness his young gun's wrath. When they got upstairs, Chico and security was in between Fernando and Yak. Yak had his hand tucked in the small of his back, which caused the rest of Fernando's team to follow suit, and reach for their guns. Fortunately all parties involved hadn't actually pulled out yet.

Gooch immediately went into action. "Didn't I tell you about bringing that bullshit into the spot?" He had Fernando hemmed up, and as soon as one of Fernando's goons sprang into action, Bundy blocked his path like a linebacker defending his quarterback. It felt as if Fernando's soldier had run smack dab into a brick wall. The sight of Bundy froze Fernando in his tracks. The ski mask Bundy had worn had no way of disguising his massive size. It was his frame that gave Fernando an air of familiarity about Bundy. Instantly, Fernando called off his dawg.

"Jose, no mas!" Fernando snatched himself away from Gooch's grip, brushing off his suit, as he griped, "Chico, what the fuck? Is this how you treat your regular custies hombre? I spend money here. Shit, I keep this hole in the wall afloat Papi! Not once have I seen these Morenos here 'til today, and you treat me as if I am the aggressor?"

"Fernando, I done told you on numerous occasions about disrespecting my place of business. As far as your money goes, you can spend it at an establishment that appreciates your business more." Chico leaned in to Fernando, "You and your friends are no longer welcome at the Player's Lounge."

Fernando spat on the floor, causing Gooch to snatch him by the collar and off of his feet, as he snarled, "You've always been a cocky son of a bitch! I'm surprised you still running around acting as if you can't be touched. Matter of fact," Gooch tossed him towards the door, "faggot ass nigga. I'm surprised you can sit your sore ass down!"

The rest of Fernando's team had no idea what Gooch was referring to. The look on Fernando's face showed that the bouncer had hit a sore spot. Fernando's eyes turned to slits that spelled murder for Gooch the next time their paths crossed. Yak glanced at Bundy, both acknowledging Gooch's slip. They didn't bother to question how Gooch knew. Chico had a look on his face that was practically apologizing from across the room.

Chapter 7

The Original Gun Clappers!

Sosa returned from Columbus, Ohio with close to forty-thousand in cash in the door panel of his 645 convertible. He couldn't wait to pull up on the block and show off the platinum diamond link chain that he'd caught another hustler for in a dice game back in Ohio. Sosa planned on trying to gas a few workers into migrating down there so he could continue to collect some of that out of town cash Columbus had to offer. He was going to make the place sound like the Holy Mecca for dealers looking to bubble. Sosa also had a big-eighth he planned on giving Yak to move. He silently hoped that Yak had the sense to go to Chico if he needed to re-up. He knew how ambitious Yak was, and couldn't picture him sitting idle when there was money to be made.

"Damn, I got a lot of news for these lil' niggas," Sosa mumbled. He would soon discover that Bundy and Yak had news of their own. When he parked his car on the block, Sosa felt a sense of pride. Murdock was bubbling like he'd never seen before, for the first time since the mid-80s. There were fiends lined up at the door to the spot waiting to get served. For a second, Sosa had to wonder if they were waiting for coke, because the last time he saw addicts lined up like that was for Heroin.

"Well, I'll be damned! Ohio must be a hell of a town Sosa." Yak was sitting in his usual spot on a crate in front of the bodega.

"You wouldn't believe it homie." Sosa pointed his chin towards the spot upstairs. "I got a lil' work for you."

"Take it upstairs. O will take care of you."

"What up wit' that bread I left you with?"

"You mean that work? Yeah, it's bread now. Like I said, go see O."

Sosa couldn't put his finger on it, but something about

the way Yak was acting and talking to him, no longer made him feel he was in charge. Sosa chose to ignore it. He hadn't bothered to call once while he was away, and knew he was out of pocket. He figured Yak was just feeling a way about his absence.

Sosa made his way upstairs, and as soon as he entered the stash house, he knew something was up. For starters, the money table where O sat counting stacks was too much for it to be the proceeds from the little bit of work he had left them with. Then he figured Chico must have hit them with a bit of consignment. That put him somewhat at ease, because Sosa knew Chico would have stipulated that such an act came with the condition that it was done in his name.

"O, what's good? From the looks of it, I gotta learn to put more faith in ya'll, huh?"

O was already schooled on what to do upon 'Sosa return. He held out his hand, and Sosa passed him a big eighth.

"Take the regular thirty off a hunned."

O said nothing. He held up a finger as if Sosa was fucking up his count. He then counted off a stack of bills and passed them to Sosa. "That's the cash owed to you before you left, and the cash for the eighth. We didn't bother to take the thirty for the workers." Then he added, "Bundy's orders!"

"Whatchu mean you ain't take out the workers pay? They plan on working for free?" Sosa tried to laugh it off, but deep down he knew the bullshit was coming.

The bullshit came in the form of Bundy waltzing through the door eating a tray full of fried rice and chicken wings from the Chinese store down the block. "What's going on O?" Sosa asked.

Bundy answered the question for Sosa. "I think in the business world they call it a Corporate Buy-Out." Bundy was licking his fingers.

"What?"

"Sosa, according to Chico, you had already agreed to give me half the block. Since you'd been gone so long, we all figured there was no possible way you still considered the block yours. I gave Yak the other half, and made O Lieutenant."

Sosa was a lot of things, but a fool wasn't one of them. Even if he had the heart to off Bundy, he knew he'd lost the workers. Now that they'd witnessed the feeling of touching real cash, they'd never go back to being spoon-fed by Sosa. He graciously bowed out. Already doing the math in his head, on the cash he had stashed in his whip, and what O had just given him. Sosa wasn't going to give Bundy the satisfaction of knowing just how much he'd hurt his pockets. Sosa grabbed the cash and quietly slid out of Bundy's and Yak's stash house. When he passed Yak outside on the crate, he didn't even make eye contact as he got in his ride and peeled off.

"So how'd he take it?"

Bundy shrugged his shoulders. "He took it."

"If you think it's gonna be a problem, I'll pop the nigga. I know where he rests his head and the whole nine. You've got the whole fam's backing on this."

"Nah, I think we good, at least for now."

Meanwhile, across town at Fernando's spot. The Spanish mob was having a meeting of their own. Fernando was at the head of the round table, as he discussed the recent events surrounding his clash with Chico at the Player's Lounge.

"I know for a fact that Chico's people are connected to the robbery at my home." Fernando banged his fist on the table. "That type of disrespect will not go unpunished!"

"How do you know it's them Fernando? I mean, can

you prove it?" one of his soldiers questioned. The question pissed Fernando off. He was in no position to give up the details without making himself look weak in front of his team. He planned on going to the grave with the secret of his violation at the hands of Melina. Instead, he switched tactics.

"Prove it? I don't have to prove shit! Loyalty gentlemen! Loyalty means moving without questioning your orders. I take loyalty and love very seriously. As you can see, Melina is no longer with us." He let the meaning of his statement linger on their minds for a few minutes before continuing, "You ask for proof Joey? You will have your proof soon enough. The Moreno bouncer at the club had a lil' slip of the tongue the other night, enough of a slip to let me know he has the information to fill in the missing piece to the puzzle." This had everyone's attention. Fernando leaned forward, whispering, "This is what we're going to do gentlemen."

Gooch sat in his vehicle parked across from the infamous rock on Farmers Boulevard and 109th. He'd been waiting on Bundy for the last half hour, and wondered if the big man was even going to show. As soon as he was ready to call it quits, the pitch black Dodge Charger pulled up beside him. Yak waved for Gooch to follow him.

Yak took Gooch to Murdock, and sure enough Bundy was spotted in the middle of the block shooting the shit with O. When he caught sight of Gooch, Bundy gave O a pound and made his way to Gooch. Gooch got out of the car, and immediately the two men started talking. Gooch wasn't sure if Yak and Bundy would want to deal with him after his slip of the tongue to Fernando the other night. It reminded him of a statement he once told one of his bouncers, his first day on the job. 'Made men don't make statements.' Now, Gooch was wishing he'd taken his own advice.

"Bundy, how're things on your end?"

"Ain't shit, just doing me, ya' know?"

Gooch looked around the block. Seeing the traffic and flow of drugs, caused Gooch to blurt out, "I see ya'll have put Fernando's money to good use, huh?" As soon as the words left his mouth, Gooch wished he could have taken them back.

"While we're on the subject, there's a few things I've got to say to you Gooch. For one, you slipped up big time mentioning what you said to Fernando." Bundy raised his hand when he saw Gooch about to explain himself.

"I know Yak told Chico what went down. You were there to hear it, but I had you pegged as the type to know when not to speak." Bundy continued to school Gooch. "Look at what you said a few minutes ago, 'ya'll have put Fernando's money to good use.' What if I was standing here with a nigga I was trying to run game on, and told him something different? You would've blown the whole scam up. It makes me hesitant to do dirt witchu."

Gooch saw that Bundy had finished his spiel, so he tried to justify his blunder. "I know I was out of pocket Bundy, but that nigga had me so pissed that I..."

"Let your emotions supersede your intelligence. And that's not a good look in our line of work," Bundy interrupted. "Lucky for you Gooch, I'm a greedy muh'fucker, therefore, I'm willing to hear you out. What's this thing you got lined up about, and what you think its worth?"

Gooch smiled. He knew that the vic he had lined up was definitely worth the time to check out. Gooch laid it all on the table. He told enough of the details for Bundy and Yak to do the jux without him, but reasoned that he had to make up for his prior mistakes.

"I was up North with this cat back in '98. Dude wasn't nobody major, but whoever his peoples were, they took good care of him. Anyway, he came in the club not too long ago, and we get to kicking it 'bout old times up in Attica. He tells me if I'm ever sick of the security gig, he could use some reliable muscle. Tells me he's got this building in the Bronx. A few apartments set up with those Hydroponic weed growing thingamajigs. He says it takes 'em a lil' over a month to gross a thirty pound crop." Gooch could see the wheels turning in Bundy's head as he continued. "He wants my security team to help him move the shit. He'll be calling me any day now."

"How we gonna pull it off if you don't know exactly when it's going down?" Bundy was looking for any holes in Gooch's plan.

"That's the best part. The nigga done showed me where the trees is going. It's a lil' spot over on Jerome Avenue." Gooch passed Bundy the address on a piece of Paper. "When I get the call, all you gotta do is be there. Afterwards, I'll just tell 'em we got robbed, and the dudes got the drop."

"I don't know Gooch. Who is this dude?"

"A nigga named Red. He's an Albino cat. You probably seen him at the club the night we got into it with Fernando and 'em." Bundy remembered the face. "I meet with the dude tomorrow night at eight. He'll give me the rest of the details then. I need to know if you're in, 'cause if not I need to find some gunslingers like yesterday."

"Fuck it. I'm in!" Then Bundy added, "Try and keep quiet 'bout this one Gooch."

Another night and no Bryce. Precious was becoming accustomed to his absence and that scared her more than anything else she could imagine happening to him on the streets. All she had to do was follow the same patterns she did while he was away up North. She sucked her teeth as she pondered the fact that Bryce hadn't even picked up on her agitation. As far as he knew, everything at home was peachy. He had begun ducking her calls, and although she had no reason to think he was creeping with another woman, playing second fiddle to the almighty dollar still made her feel a way. Precious looked at the clock, and saw that it was one-thirty in the morning. She took a blanket out of the linen closet, and an extra pillow and placed them on the couch for Bryce.

Gooch had just gotten off the phone with Red. After discovering the exact time and date for the drop, Gooch called Bundy. Red hadn't been the trusting fool Gooch thought he was. Gooch found that once he committed to being Red's security, the Albino horticulturist gave him the real address to where he wanted the weed to be delivered. It was still on Jerome Avenue, only the actual address was one building over. After informing Bundy of the change in plans, Bundy felt more secure about it. The original plan Gooch gave seemed too easy, but with the changes, he had reason to believe Red was now comfortable enough for the jux to go off without a hitch.

Gooch hung up the phone in Chico's office, and got ready to call it a night. He went into Chico's desk and hit the button that exposed the hidden mini bar behind the couch and poured himself a shot of Patron. He wanted to go over some last minute details with Bundy before the following night came. He was in such a rush when he exited the Player's Lounge he never saw Fernando's henchmen slumped back in the corner of the club.

Bleep, Bleep! Gooch's car alarm chirped. As he went to open the door, everything went black. The last thing the barely conscious bouncer could recall was the sound of his own car trunk being slammed on top of him. By the time Gooch's senses returned, he was fully aware of what was happening to him. He silently wondered if Red had somehow gotten word of his plot to rob him. His mind started playing through the possibilities, but he had done what Bundy had instructed him to do and told no one. He couldn't think of any other beefs he had. At least none that amounted to the type of trouble his abductors were going through. Finally; he felt his car come to a halt. His heart rate started to increase, feeling like it was ready to jump out of his chest. Gooch was glad to discover he wasn't handcuffed. He knew whoever was responsible for his kidnapping wasn't bluffing, so as soon as the trunk popped open, the burly bouncer planned to go out swinging.

Gooch heard a few voices outside of the trunk and noticed that one of the men had a slight accent in his speech. As soon as it hit him, the trunk flew open. Gooch popped up swatting and swinging, but there was no one within his reach. By the time he was upright, he was staring down the barrel of over a half dozen semi-automatic weapons. Behind them he could make out a shadow of a grinning face. The street lamp above silhouetted the face providing only an outline of the person. Although he couldn't make out the person's identity, Gooch could see that the leader of the pack was smiling at him.

"I believe we have some unfinished business, com-padre."

"Awww fuck!" Gooch groaned.

"Not yet Papi. Not yet." It was the last thing Gooch heard.

For all the drug dealers Bundy had robbed in his life. All the home invasions and drug spots he'd taken. All the thugs he'd extorted, smacked, and violated. All the times he'd let violence overcome him. All the penitentiaries he'd ruled with an iron fist, one would think Bundy hadn't a fear in the world. Yet, a simple look of disappointment on Precious' face scared him more than any beef he had ever encountered. It was the main reason he now found himself tip-toeing through the house at three in the morning with his boots in hand.

As soon as he placed his ear to their bedroom door, Precious called out, "Don't even bother Bryce. Your dinner's in the microwave and the linen on the couch is for you."

Bundy didn't even bother to question her. He knew he was pressing his luck. At the same time, he was more relieved that she'd chosen to have him sleep on the couch than face him herself. He had no idea how he was going to explain his actions. He'd already promised more times than he could count, that he'd stop roaming the streets and make it home at a decent hour. On more than one occasion Precious found herself having to lie to Bryce's Parole Officer that he was out somewhere working overtime.

Bryce was sitting on the couch picking over his dinner. While Bundy mentally planned for the upcoming jux on Red. An hour had passed and Precious couldn't take it anymore. She stepped out of the bedroom to confront her man. Precious sat on the couch and said nothing. Bryce looked at her expecting a confrontation but she simply stared at the television as if she was waiting on him to break the tension. Just when he thought he might be in the clear, Precious spoke. "What are you doing out there Bryce?"

"Out where?"

"In the streets Bryce. Out there in the streets."

"C'mon Precious, I'm working. Sometimes I get a few gigs on the side."

"So you're just going to lie to me like I'm your P.O.?"

Precious folded her arms. "So what kind of side job allows you to give away fifteen grand, huh?"

"First of all, I'm not giving away fifteen grand. I'm giving it to you." Bundy tried the ole' get on the defensive routine with Precious.

"Whatever Bryce, just in case you think you can buy love and loyalty, I'm telling you upfront, I'm not doing any more bids with you! You get locked up; you're on your own."

For a few seconds there was complete silence. When Precious saw that Bryce had no response, she got up and made her way to the bedroom. When she reached the door, she spun around. With tears brimming at the corners of her eye, she said, "At the rate they're killing black men on the streets, I'd like to think you had more sense than you're showing Bryce. They killed that man Shawn Bell for nothing, and you think you've got a chance out there with your record. If that were you, your rap sheet would make it that much easier for them to justify murdering you out there. And that's just worrying about the law. Then you got all these thugs you probably out starting shit with." Precious sucked her teeth, adding, "As we speak, somebody you know is more than likely two steps from being murdered, and you're just following them to

an early grave like it can't happen to big ole' Bundy."
Precious slammed the door, as he waved her off. Neither
Bryce nor Precious had any idea how true her words were.

Splash! The bucket of freezing cold water woke Gooch
up immediately. When he looked up and saw Fernando
grinning at him, his heart fell into the pit of his stomach.
He was hoping that the last few hours had been nothing
more than a bad dream. Sure enough, his restraints proved
otherwise.

"Buenos Dias, Cabron." Fernando smacked Gooch
twice across the face. Gooch started tugging at the piano
wire which cut into the flesh on his wrists and ankles.
Fernando leaned into Gooch until he was so close he could
see tiny beads of sweat dripping from his pores. "I can't
hear a word you're speaking Gooch. You have to learn to
stop mumbling," Fernando taunted.

"Miguel!" Fernando called on one of his most trusted
soldiers. He patted Gooch on the head, while ordering,
"Go and get the torture toys."

Gooch started going crazy. He shook and bounced the
wooden chair he was strapped to so violently; it threatened

to crack under his weight. "Muva'foonka!"

Even through the duct tape, Fernando knew Gooch was cursing him out.

"I know Papi, I know. It's a scary feeling having your life in another's hands. My dear Melina begged for her life too." Then Fernando's whole demeanor changed and he got aggressive. "If I didn't spare her, what makes you think your filthy ass stands a chance?" Fernando hocked up a glob of phlegm from his throat, and spat in Gooch's face.

"Gooch, you are going to tell me what I need to know. The question is, how much pain are you willing to endure before you do so?" Gooch started pulling on his restraints a second time, causing even more damage to himself. At that moment, Miguel came into the room tugging a duffle bag full of tools. He placed the bag by Fernando's feet, as Fernando continued to explain the situation to Gooch. "I was never one for the whole torture thing. That is mi amigo's area of expertise. I'm going to leave you two here for a while so you can get acquainted. When I return, we'll see if you are ready to answer any questions."

As soon as Fernando left the room, Miguel went to work. He was meticulous in his methods. He showed no emotions as he dug out a hammer and chisel, walked over to Gooch, and hacked off his big toe in one fluid motion.

"Mmrrph! Hmmr!" Gooch rocked back and forth a few times before he passed out. The duct tape muffled his screams, almost causing him to choke in the process.

Jerome Ave., Bronx N.Y.

Bundy checked the address Gooch had given him for the second time. The building before him was similar to the stash house he and Yak had on Murdock Avenue, except Red's stash house sat above a dilapidated Chinese restaurant. Bundy sat in the courtyard across from the spot eating his trademark four chicken wings and fried rice.

Cheap muh'fuckers never give up enough duck sauce. He sucked his teeth, and was about to make his way back to the restaurant to pay the five cents he knew the owner would ask for in exchange for extra sauce. That's when he saw him.

Gooch's description of Red was right on point. The heavyset Albino man with a dirt blond nappy blowout was making his way towards an all black Cadillac Escalade. Bundy waited for him to pull off before trailing behind him in his Dodge Charger.

Gooch sat in the chair with his head slumped in his lap. Every time he tried to doze off to relieve the pain in his body, Miguel slapped him awake. When he looked up towards the only source of light in the room, the bare bulb threatened to blind him. He had an I.V. tube supplying him just enough morphine to keep him alive until Fernando was done with him. Tears ran down Gooch's face as he saw the bandages on his left hand where his ring finger used to be. The throbbing sensation coupled with the blood stain was the only reason Gooch was aware of the amputation. His right arm held a trail of cigarette burns that led up to his neck, and every fingernail on his right hand had been torn from the root. It was over an hour ago that Gooch had come to the realization that he was going to die. Now, he just wished Fernando's goon would get it over with.

"Just kill me," Gooch murmured. It was a hoarse whisper that was barely audible. Miguel had long ago removed the duct tape from Gooch's mouth in order to give him enough oxygen to prolong his torture. Miguel said nothing. He'd been trained by the military in the art of breaking a man's will, so when Gooch responded, he did as he was instructed and hit the send button on his cell phone to inform Fernando that their captive was temporarily conscious.

When Fernando entered the room, he got right to the point. "I have to admit you are an admirable foe. I would have thought you'd break by now Papi. How do you do it?" Fernando raised his hands to the air as if he had an audience, "In such a gloomy situation, what is it that could possibly keep you from telling me what I need to know? Is it loyalty?" Fernando heard a whisper so low he had to get right up on Gooch.

"What's that?" Gooch was babbling, but Fernando was able to make out the last few words 'going to kill me anyway.' As Fernando started nodding his head Gooch jerked forward and bit into his ear.

"Aarrrggh!" Fernando's scream brought Miguel to his aid, but not before Gooch ripped off a chunk of Fernando's ear as a souvenir. Miguel put the Colt .45 to the base of Gooch's skull as Gooch started to laugh uncontrollably.

"No!" Miguel lifted his thumb off the hammer and eased the pistol away from its target. Fernando, with a handkerchief on his ear, started grinning along with Gooch's hysterical giggles. "It feels good doesn't it

amigo? You know, revenge." Gooch stopped laughing, his
eyes showing pure hatred.

"You seem to be a smart man. I'm going to, as you
say, play it straight with you." Fernando threw the rag to
the side and ignored the blood dripping onto his Brookes
Brothers suit. "You are definitely going to die. Tell me
what I need to know, and I will give you my word on two
things." For one, Fernando pulled out a blue steel .357
with a four inch barrel, "your death will be quick. One
to the head, bang!" Fernando mushed Gooch's forehead
with the barrel of the snub nose. "And two," he dug into
his pocket and pulled out his trump card, "I will spare
your family. On that I swear."

When Gooch looked up, Fernando was showing him
a picture of his wife picking up his two daughters from
school. Gooch went nuts, as Fernando ordered Miguel out
of the room. With just the two of them there, Fernando
hit him with the last real conversation Gooch would ever
have.

"Papi, we gangsters, right? So, you know women and
kids have no business in our business, si?" Fernando
leaned in to whisper, this time making sure to stay out of
Gooch's reach. "You know what those robbers did to me,
even worse, by my own Melina! I'll miss her Papi, but

please don't force me to go against my beliefs and harm the babies. You dying anyway, so be a man."

When Gooch thought about it, he didn't have many options. He was going to die, and would never be around to know if Fernando carried through with his promise or was bluffing.

I've gambled with my life for decades. I can't gamble wit' my babies' lives, Gooch thought. All of a sudden, he started nodding his head. Tears flew as he moaned too numb to actually sob.

"You manned up Papi. You are a true warrior. I salute you." As soon as Gooch gave Fernando the information he was looking for, the Spanish mobster stayed true to his word by giving Gooch a quick death by a single shot to the head.

When Red finally pulled over, Bundy saw that it was the spot that Gooch had originally been told was the drop point. By the way the men were acting, Bundy figured they had something in the works, and would be contacting Gooch sometime in the very near future.

Shit, I might've hit the jackpot here. You know the

ole' stick-up kid's rule of thumb nigga. Bundy said the old jailhouse saying aloud; "If you watch a nigga long enough, you can always find an area where he's lax at. Then, it's stickin' & movin' baby, stickin' & movin'!"

Change The Game!
Chapter 8

Murdock Ave.

With Sosa out of the picture; Yak was officially the man. Bundy, not caring for the lack of instant gratification that came with drug dealing, gave Yak free reign to do as he pleased with the block. Everyone in their circle knew Bundy's presence was more so that of a figurehead. Yak was the one out there on the daily grind making it happen.

Lately, the block had been so busy, Bundy and Yak barely saw each other. Neither sweated the other's absence, because both had gotten what they wanted out of the deal. Even O was starting to come up in the game. He had stacked himself a few gees copping a bit of weight from Yak, and wholesaling it to a few dealers he knew in Long Island. Everyone was eating. The women were plentiful, and the whole clique down to the soldiers, were happy.

On this particular day, Yak was going the extra mile. He had the George Foreman grill on the side of the building where he and his team were throwing a 'poor man's barbeque.' Yak was in the process of turning over a few steaks when a kid named Timmy rolled up on a miniature battery powered Cadillac Escalade his mom had purchased at Toy's 'R' Us.

"Yo Yak! Whussup?" At age five, Timmy's mother had him emulating the hustlers on Murdock Avenue. She didn't know any better. Her man was an old school cat named Clay, who was nearing the end of a ten year stint in the Feds. Joanna thought that by dressing Timmy in the latest Jordan's, and allowing him to hang around the Murdock mob, she was raising him in the same fashion that had molded Timmy's father, Clay. Had Joanna paid more attention to the letters Clay was writing her, she would have discovered that Clay had outgrown the streets and wanted more for their son.

"Whatchu mean what's up, lil' nigga? What you want to be up?" Yak dropped his spatula, and threw his hands up to Timmy as they play fought. It tickled Yak to see the little guy throw on his ice grill, and do his childlike version of the infamous '52 hand blocks.' A boxing style some say derived from a handful of the most gifted prison pugilists.

Timmy did a spin and shot out a two piece that Yak could have easily avoided, but let connect just to egg Timmy on. It was their regular routine. Yak had come up under Clay. It was Clay who schooled him to the art of the hustle. After Clay's federal bid, Bundy became the closest thing Yak had to replacing Clay.

"Oooh...go lil' Clay," two of Yak's workers bigged up Timmy's technique. Yak threw a jab that Timmy sidestepped. He could see the pride in the youngster's face.

"Timmy, knock it off." Joanna stood to the side laughing at Yak and his acting skills. When Yak looked up, Joanna pointed. "Yak, you gon' fuck around and burn them steaks."

"Oh shit!" Yak ran to the grill to flip the steaks. "Jo, how you like your steak?" Yak and Joanna went back to her days as Jo Jo. He was the only one besides Clay who was allowed to call her that. The name had too much history behind it for just anyone to refer to her by it. It dated back to the mid-eighties, when Joanna was the boss' wifey.

"Well done Yak. You know how us black folk do, burn the edges of fat on that muh'fucker," Joanna laughed.

"Know that's right," Yak agreed.

"Yak, lemme get a soda." Yak laughed, knowing Timmy wasn't asking. Yak reached into the cooler to get Timmy a soda, and that's when all hell broke loose. Two cars appeared from opposite sides of the street, blocking Yak in. By the time the first shot was fired, Yak looked to his right and saw that Joanna had snatched Timmy up. They was hiding in the enclave at the entrance of the stash house. Yak's soldiers immediately returned fire. It seemed that the unknown gunmen were taken by surprise. One of the gunmen concentrated solely on Yak as the others tried their best to keep the soldiers at bay.

To the surprise of the obsessed gunslinger, Yak's hands came out of the garbage can gripping two fully auto Ruger P90's with extended thirty shot clips. Yak's crew always teased him about the guns being overkill. At the present moment, members of the Murdock Squad was thankful for Yak's fascination with high powered artillery. The Ruger backed up the intruders with a fusillade of half a dozen shots from a mere tap of the trigger.

"Uh-uh muh'fuckers. Don't run now!" Yak barked. He moved forward as if he had a death wish. As the drama ensued, Yak remembered the one thing Bundy had always instilled in him. 'In real life, a shootout is nothing like the movies. It feels like twenty minutes, but only lasts for one, so make those sixty seconds count.' Yak kept that in mind. Showing the intruder's that he wasn't afraid of dying. He leapt over a parked car and dumped three shots into one of his rivals, killing him instantly. The death of one of them gave Yak's team the heart to back down the other two as they were forced to shoot around the corner blindly at their targets.

Kling! Klak! A slug ricocheted off a brick in front of one of the violators. While Yak's two soldiers banged it out, Yak kept a steady stream of artillery at the occupants of the second vehicle. One got hit, and it caused the driver to put the car in reverse. Yak's next shot blew out the rear tire causing the vehicle to crash into a pole. Not even thirty seconds in, and the visiting group of bandits started to retreat. They could hear sirens approaching, and that's when fate turned towards the other team's advantage.

One of Yak's soldiers caught a slug in the shoulder, which caused his partner to start fleeing. The gun slid from the wounded man's hand toward the entrance where Joanna and Timmy sat crouched for cover. Joanna feared for her and her son's safety, but Timmy was too young to fully understand what he was witnessing. Timmy leapt from Joanna's embrace, and ran to pass Yak the gun.

"Yak!" he called out, thinking he was coming to his big homie's rescue.

"Timmy!" Joanna's scream caused Yak to peep the confusion from his peripheral. The gunman grinned, knowing by Yak's wide-eyed expression that the young boy was someone important in Yak's life. As the triggerman leveled his weapon at Yak, his partner fired an array of shots towards Yak before he could get a bead on his partner. Yak did just as the gunmen hoped and jumped in front of Timmy; shielding him while dumping three shots in one of the men's torsos.

"Go to your mother!" Yak yelled grimacing as a bullet tore through his leg. Two more shots whizzed past Yak. The shots were so close he could hear them whistle past him with a cracking sound. He knew it was only a matter of time before one of the hollow points found its mark in a vital organ.

"Fucking cowards!" Yak barked, popping Hydra Shock slugs from one gun, and Black Rhinos from another. Yak knew the men were using Timmy to their advantage, and by their sloppy marksmanship, knew under different circumstances he would have ended their standoff already.

In the chaos and confusion, young Timmy ran out into the street instead of to the safety of his mother. Yak reached out to grab him, and that's when his luck came to an end. As Yak swung around to toss Timmy to Joanna, the main gunner stepped out and fired dead at Yak's chest. His instincts somehow knew it was the shot that would floor him. Yak did the only thing possible, and cuffed Timmy into his chest as he took the slugs in his back. Yak smiled as he looked Joanna in the eyes. Her eyes said it all. She embraced Timmy, grateful that her lil' man was unscathed. As the two ran off, Yak could feel a shadow over him blocking out the sun, and when he turned, was surprised to see Fernando grinning down at him.

"Admirable thing you did compadre. There just might be a heaven for a G, huh?" It was the last thing Yak heard before Fernando squeezed the trigger.

"Another jux?" Chico smacked himself in the head and did a double take of Bundy sitting at his desk. He couldn't believe Bundy was acting all nonchalant, as if what he'd just proposed was the most logical thing in the world. "Bundy, you straight. What the fuck do you need another jux for?"

"I'm straight? Chico, you the one that's bugging if you think that lil' bit of chump change makes me straight. You're the one that's straight. That's why you ain't trying to ride for the cause wit' a nigga. You already eating."

Bundy's statement hurt Chico's pride. Here he was risking his clientele on the one shark in the guppy pond, and the predator wanted *all* the fish in the pond. It was the analogy Chico spat that had jump started their current debate. "You're fucking tripping B. You'll never feel straight for the simple fact that you're doing the juxes without any type of goal in mind. You have no plan. Without a goal you're simply chasing a carrot on a stick. And you're the donkey, motivated by any opportunity for quick cash. How can you be content, if you don't know what'll make you content?" Chico reached into his desk drawer and pulled out another check for Bundy.

When he looked at it, he realized the check was almost double the normal amount. "What's this, a raise?"

Chico took a deep breath before answering. "They found Gooch's body this morning. I don't know what he went and got himself into, and to be honest, I don't think I wanna know." He paused before saying his next statement. "I'm giving you his position if you want it. Being that you think I'm against you and all. I figure you may not want it. If you do take it Bundy, don't make me regret it."

Bundy was no longer listening. He wondered if Gooch's sudden demise was connected to Red in anyway. *I followed that nigga all day yesterday,* he thought, dismissing his theory. His logic was clouded by the fact that he could pluck Red's pocket without having to give Gooch a cut.

God must have sent an angel to look over Yak. Fernando's bullet shattered on the concrete two inches from his head. When Yak saw Fernando stumble back a few steps, he thought the Latin Capo was steadying himself for a second shot. That's when Yak heard the next shot that caused his adversary to flee. He heard Fernando's getaway cars screech down the street, as someone grabbed his guns and passed them to Joanna.

"Put these in your crib." Yak heard the voice of his trusted lieutenant. O pulled out his cell and began explaining to the barely conscious Yak. "Cops are damn near here. The 911 call makes us look like innocent civilians."

By the time the cops turned onto the block. Joanna was putting pressure on Yak's wound, while O spoke with the 911 operator.

"Yes, Ma'am, the officers have arrived." O made sure the cops heard him. He knew he was pressing his luck, but had no intention of leaving Yak to die. Lucky for Yak, Fernando had used a Magnum, so the slug went straight through. He heard one of the EMT's mention that had it been a small caliber weapon, he might not have been so lucky.

Not even fifteen minutes after the incident, O and Joanna were taken to the 113th precinct for questioning. The two detectives working the case were Roberts and Jones.

Jones was a no-nonsense type who could smell bullshit a mile away. It was no wonder that he immediately doubted the two witnesses' recollections of what had transpired on Murdock Avenue.

Joanna and O sat in separate interrogation rooms. After an hour of intense questioning, Roberts entered the room where his partner had O and motioned for him to step outside. Before he could leave, O asked "Is this going to take much longer Detective? I would like to visit the hospital to make sure my friend is alright."

"We're almost done here. If you want, I can check on his condition for you." O nodded, while Jones did his best not to treat O like the suspect he was.

Outside the room, Jones and Roberts began discussing their theories. "What do you think?" Roberts asked.

"I think the whole story is a load of crap. The patient is T. Branch a.k.a. Yak. He has a minor record and is known as one of the hustlers on that block by the task force. He tested positive for GSR, so we know he was one of the gunmen. Problem is, we can't prove it. "Whatchu think?"

Roberts pulled out his scratch pad, analytical as always. "I agree with you whole heartedly. But this girl says the guy Yak saved her child's life. Between that, and the other guy dialing 911, I seriously doubt we'd even get the Grand Jury to indict." Roberts saw the disgusted look on Jones' face, and added, "You've gotta realize Paul, our gut instinct and the evidence are two different things." He flipped his pad to another page. "We've got proof that two cars were opposite each other. Now my gut tells me the perps tried to box the kid in. A decent Defense Attorney could argue that this was merely two factions settling a dispute, and that Yak," he flipped his pad again, "according to this Joanna girl, was simply walking home and got caught in the middle. By the time she tells of the heroic sacrifice Yak made for her five year old, there might not be a dry eyed juror in the room. Shit, they might even catch an attitude with us for even having the audacity to charge the guy. He'll be a fucking Saint! Jesus won't have squat on this guy once his mouthpiece is done."

Jones held up his hand. "I get the point Roberts. So, what now? We just let him go?"

Roberts let out a long breath of frustration. "We keep an eye on the area. These guys aren't done, so I'm sure their enemies will make another attempt. The kid is in the recovery unit, and according to the doctors, he ain't going nowhere any time soon. Until then, let's see what we can dig up."

When Yak awoke, he was in the Intensive Care Unit of Jamaica Hospital. The doctors were in the process of explaining his condition to Candy. Precious consoled her, while Bundy and O listened from afar. Joanna sat to the side on a bench, while Timmy kept his face pressed to the window staring at Yak.

"We're going to keep an overnight watch on him here, and if his progress keeps up, we'll move him to a regular room first thing in the morning. He's listed in critical condition for now, but it's a miracle that he isn't far worse off than he is."

"Can we see him?" Candy asked.

"I'll give you a few minutes, but after that you'll have to let him get his rest."

They entered the room, and Yak must have felt their presence; he turned to face them. "Oh man baby," Candy kissed him softly on the forehead, "you had me scared to death." All Yak could managed was a weak smile.

"Glad to have you with us Yak." O winked, as he nodded his head towards the window. When Yak looked, he saw Detectives Roberts and Jones turn their heads as soon as he glanced their way.

Joanna nudged her son Timmy. "Um...thanks Yak." Timmy stared at the floor as he wrung his hands.

"For what lil' man?" Yak's voice was a hoarse whisper. Candy got him a glass of water from the nightstand next to his bed.

"Saving my life?" Timmy shrugged his shoulders, still unsure of the events he'd witnessed earlier.

"Don't thank me Timmy. Shoot, if I'd let something happen to you, your Pops would have killed me anyway." Yak tried to make light of the situation. "Yo O! Love and loyalty baby boy." Yak coughed, causing Candy to worry.

"You alright baby?" Yak nodded.

Everything was going smooth until Bundy spoke. "You know who did this to you?"

Yak nodded. "Fernando."

"Don't even sweat it, I'm on it." Upon hearing her man, Precious sucked her teeth and left the room. Bundy didn't bother chasing after her because he meant exactly what he said. "Yo, I'm gonna come through when you're more up to the visits. I'll leave you in the ladies' hands." Bundy glanced around the room, smiling. He knew Yak was always a ladies man and would milk the attention. "Yeah, you'll be aight!"

On his way out, Bundy and Precious locked eyes. At the same time, the elevator opened and Bundy walked in without so much as an acknowledgement. Before the door could fully close, O was right on his heels, he hopped in. "I know it's going down. I don't plan on missing out on any of the action."

"Finally! This is one paranoid nigga. I ain't never think this thing was going down." Red's crew was loading up the weed in a white mini van. Bundy and O sat slumped across the street in the Dodge Charger.

"This is some real bullshit B! All this shit ain't even necessary."

"You wanted in, right? So stop bitching. You's in nigga!"

O's gripe stemmed from the fact that Bundy had him dressed up like somebody's grandmother. He wore a big black church crown, and an oversized black dress that hid his stocky muscular frame. Bundy even had him decked out in some all white orthopedic nurse shoes. Bundy glanced at O and couldn't help but snicker.

"Damn Grandma. You always bitching 'bout I don't

spend no time with you, and now that I do, you still complaining." O gave Bundy the middle finger.

Across the street, Red and his goons piled into the mini van and drove off. O and Bundy followed behind them. Once they reached the building on Jerome Avenue, Bundy got out of his car and pretended to help his grandmother into the building. O's disguise was the only way that the two of them could get right up on Red without raising the dealer's suspicion. As they went to head up the stairs, Red stopped one of his workers.

"Puma, what are you doing?" Red gave his man Puma a look that suggested he be a gentleman for once in his life. Allow the elderly woman to go up the stairs first.

"Huh? Oh, pardon me." He nodded in Bundy's direction. O cracked a smile underneath the thin veil hiding his goatee. When they reached the second landing of the staircase, Bundy and O took their time turning the corner. They were unsure of which floor Red's stash house was located. Red turned towards the only door at the end of the hall and stuck his key in the door, and that's when Bundy and O sprang into action.

"Don't move muh'fuckers!" Bundy mumbled, not wanting any neighbors to hear the ruckus and notify the authorities. O pulled off his hat standing in a bowlegged shooting stance snarling, "And don't turn this robbery into a homicide by trying some dumb shit!" It took all of Bundy's strength not to burst out laughing at the sight. O had to use the barrel of his gun to pull the wedgie out of his ass from where the dress had ridden up on him.

"Get in the crib!" Bundy nodded as he used his Desert Eagle to point towards the entrance to the spot. Immediately after they entered the apartment, O used wire to secure Red to the nearest chair, while Bundy handcuffed his goons to the radiator.

"We can make this real quick, or slow and painful. It's your call. Now, where's the money at Red?" Red was surprised at the fact Bundy referred to him by name. When O opened the duffle bag the men were carrying, sure enough, thirty pounds of weed sat staring them in the face.

"This is it right there. Ya'll got it all. I didn't get a chance to move the shit yet."

Bundy started shaking his head and pulled out a nail gun from his backpack, "Wrong answer, Red." He shot Red in the hand with the nail gun while O duct taped his mouth in mid scream. "Normally I don't do this, but since somebody done killed the homie, I'll make it easier for you." Bundy looked Red dead in the eye, and broke down the facts to him. "Gooch done gave you up nigga, so I know you're supposed to drop the weed off and pick up the cash. I'll even go so far as admitting that we know about your lil' hydroponic weed set."

Bundy smacked the shit out of Red. The slap stung so much it made Red's eyes water. He struggled at first but noticed the nail in his hand stopped him from struggling any further. O picked up the nail gun and shot the other hand. By then, Red was spilling his guts through the duct tape. Bundy snatched off the tape.

"The money's in the freezer, top left corner." Red nodded towards the 'fridge.

"You did good Red." Sure enough the cash was right where Red said it would be. They were neatly stacked in ten thousand dollar rows, and appeared to be about $160,000.

"That's what the fuck I'm talking 'bout," O barked. As the two of them began packing up Red's money and drugs, the Albino hustler summoned up the courage to mouth off at the stick-up duo.

"Look at 'em. All excited over a mere month's work. I swear to God, I can't stand ya'll stick up kids. Find a hustle nigga. Get yo' own!"

Bundy took Red's comment in stride. The way he saw

it, he'd paid over a hundred grand to pop off fly at the mouth, while most did it for free. O on the other hand, wasn't as tolerant. He felt Red's statement in the pit of his stomach. Red's words made him feel like a thirsty derelict. *I got sum'thin' for that ass, yellow muh'fucker!* O thought.

"You ready Grandma?" O flipped Bundy the bird for a second time. "Aight, we out!"

Before they left Red's spot, O stopped in front of the herbal horticulturist. "You don't like stick-up kids, huh? Well I don't like hustlers. I rob niggas like ya'll 'cause I figure ya'll can't call police. And what you muh'fuckers go and do as soon as you get loose, but call police." O raised the nail gun to Red's crotch, adding, "In the words of P-Diddy, 'Take that! Take that!'" He fired three nails into Red's manhood.

Bundy wasted no time making his way to Queens Boulevard. When he got to the car lot, Tina came out to greet him. O sat stuffing his Grandma outfit in the duffle bag before tossing it in the back seat.

"What up nigga? You got a problem wit' the Charger?"

"Nah, I'm here for that trade in we talked about."

Bundy turned to O "and my man is looking to cop a lil' sum'thin too." O began browsing the lot, while Tina followed behind Bundy.

"Business must be good, huh?" Tina grinned a knowing smile that seemed to bother Bundy for some reason.

"It's aight." Bundy shrugged, stopping in front of a Platinum Grey 2008 Range Rover.

"You like that?"

"How much?" Bundy ignored her question, as Tina quoted the sticker price.

"He wants sixty. It's practically new." Bundy was disappointed that Tina would try and beat him in the head. He was well aware of the fact that mostly all of the car dealers on Hillside Avenue and Queens Boulevard bought their cars from the out of State Federal Auctions for a third of their blue book value. They repaired the minor damage at a body shop affiliated with their lot, only to turn around and sell them to hustlers in the 'hood for the suggested retail price.

Bundy pointed to a 5series BMW in navy blue. "What if I'm buying the Beemer too?" The owner of the lot overheard him, and immediately decided to intervene.

"I got him Tina. You can help the other young man out." Tina hesitated at first, but saw that she had no wins.

The owner was trying to avoid paying her such a high commission, while Tina's mind was calculating a scam on a much larger scale.

"I'll give you both of them for eighty."

"Done! But I'll be trading that," he pointed towards the Charger, "as well as dropping thirty cash. You cool wit' that?"

"No problem my friend."

O had picked out a pearl white Jaguar XK8. As they all went into the trailer to discuss the paperwork, Bundy couldn't help but notice Tina all up in his business. Before he could figure out the reason, the owner of the lot had solved it for him.

"Okay, so you put down four thousand on the Charger. What I can..."

"You mean eight thousand, don't you? I put eight on the Charger." When he looked up at Tina, the way she turned her head spelled it out for Bundy. Tina had pocketed fifty percent of his down payment. Bundy smiled. Being a thief himself, he knew the logic behind her larcenous act.

"It says right here...four thousand." The owner pointed to the screen.

"Oh yeah, I had changed my mind at the last minute, My bad." Bundy thought to himself, *I get it Tee! What were the chances of me ever noticing? Probably thought I'd have paid off too much to notice by the time I came back for a trade in. By then, you could've accounted for losing four gee's by talking some interest shit.* Bundy grinned winking at Tina as if to say; 'We'll talk later.'

He really didn't care one way or the other, he just didn't want to raise the owner's suspicion and cause him to back out of the deal he and O were getting. By the time Bundy and O dropped the cash on the table, the owner was already juggling the paperwork so that it would coincide with Bundy's pay stubs from the club. Tina almost jumped out her seat when she overheard Bundy say that the BMW would be going to his fiancée Precious.

"If you guys come back in a few hours, I can have you hooked up with some temp plates so you can cruise them bad boys today." They gave the owner dap, and Bundy took his business card. From that day forward he knew he'd be doing business with the owner as opposed to Tina.

Tina was in the living room of her crib, pacing back and forth. She knew that her and Bundy went way back. She had to wonder if what they once had superseded a four grand theft. Normally, Tina would have simply asked Bundy for the money, but after almost five years, and him just coming home, she figured he might not have had it to spare. It didn't help that during his prison stint she had only bothered to answer one of his letters. Tina wondered if she could explain how rough the last four years and three months of her life had been to the big man.

Tina had a four year old daughter who stayed with her mother. She was scamming welfare by acting as if her daughter Brianna lived with her. Lucky for Tina, all her mother cared about was her granddaughter's well being. She never pestered Tina concerning the food stamp card, or small amount of monthly stipends the State allowed her. In order to keep up with her fast lifestyle, Tina rented Brianna's room out to her homegirl Michelle, a stripper who grew up with her back when she lived on Springfield Boulevard and 112th Avenue.

All of a sudden, the doorbell rang, causing Tina to jump. "Girl, what the hell is wrong with you? You been acting all jittery and shit." Michelle got up to answer the door, when Tina stopped her. "Hold up, I think..."

Michelle side stepped her. "Will you calm down? That ain't nothing but the pizza I ordered an hour ago." Michelle strutted towards the door in a slip, and some WalMart slippers that looked like they belonged to a child. The doggie ears on her slippers flip flopped with each step she took. When the delivery man got a glimpse of Michelle's body, she smiled, knowing he was a potential trick and didn't even know it. When he glanced past her, his face said it all. He took in the filthy mess the two girls called a living room; empty milk cartons were strewn across the coffee table; old cartons of Chinese food were stuffed with the loose tobacco of half a dozen Dutch Master Cigars.

Tina's crib was the neighborhood crash spot. It was where all the hustlers around the way came to in the wee hours of the morning. It wasn't the girls' looks that had all of them coming to visit. It was more so the fact that there weren't too many other women who had nothing better to do than blow trees with the block huggers working the third shift on a hot summer night. Most of them had girlfriends who were about something. Tina's crib was the hangout when things got slow and they needed a break. Even Michelle was absent from the equation until around four A.M., when she usually came strutting in the house after stripping all night. Tina was the only one who had nothing going for her except the occasional scam that came so rarely, by the time she scored, it was just enough for her to get back to square one.

Michelle paid the deliveryman, but when she tried to close the door, Bundy's foot prevented her from doing so. When she looked up and saw the gargantuan frame he possessed, Michelle blushed, wondering if every part of Bundy came in size 5X.

"Hey cutie, is Tina home?"

She eyed Bundy from head to toe then glanced at his Platinum Range, before calling out, "Tina! You got company at the door."

When Tina saw that it was Bundy at the door, her heart fell. "Um...let's talk in my bedroom." Bundy had an evil smirk on his face. Seeing Tina nervous had him slightly aroused. As soon as the two entered her bedroom, Tina tried to give Bundy her lame excuse.

"Bundy I know I was wrong..." Bundy held up a hand, silencing her in her tracks.

"I'm willing to offer you a lil' proposition, and by the look of shorty at the door, the pot just sweetened a bit."

Tina was all ears. She was just happy she wasn't about to feel the big man's wrath. She knew from experience what Bundy was capable of when he felt he was slighted.

"You owe me four grand Tee. I'll tell you what. If you get your girl to let me knock ya'll off in a threesome, I might be willing to let your lil' slick ass slide without paying your debt."

Tina's mind started grinding out the possibilities of Bundy's proposal. She had no problem with it, but knew she couldn't speak for Michelle. "Gimme a minute Bundy." When Tina opened her bedroom door, Michelle jumped back, giving away the fact that she was eavesdropping.

"Uh, what's up?" Michelle knew she was caught, but she also knew that Tina needed her help and was in no position to start beefing. What Tina hadn't known was that Michelle was a freak. She just knew how to keep her personal business to herself. Michelle was already turning tricks in the VIP section of most of the clubs she worked at. Bundy's proposal wouldn't be much of a shock to her at all.

"Listen 'Chelle. I don't know how much of that you heard, or if you heard it at all, but I'm in a bit of a jam." Tina sat on the couch, as Michelle followed suit, doing the same. "That big ass nigga in my bedroom is named Bundy. I knew this cat before I went and shitted on him during his bid. I know I was wrong, but I wasn't trying to do no bid wit' a nigga who already had a girl he planned on coming home to."

"No doubt!"

Tina stopped her before she could get sidetracked.

"That's not it." she took a deep breath before telling Michelle, "I stole four grand from the nigga, and he wants to collect. I ain't got time to get into the particulars of it...."

This time Michelle cut Tina off. "I don't have that type of cash Tee, and even if I did, how would you pay it back?"

"He doesn't want the money 'Chelle. He wants a threesome." Tina braced herself for Michelle's reaction before continuing, "and he wants you to be the third party."

Michelle had to let the words sink in, so there was a moment of silence before she answered. "Let me speak to him for a minute." Tina thought she just might have a chance, so she waved towards her room, giving Michelle the go ahead. When Michelle entered the room, Bundy smiled.

"You spoke to Tina?" Michelle nodded. Bundy could have sworn he saw a trace of a smile on Michelle's lips.

"So you probably think I'm bugging, huh?"

"Depends." Michelle shrugged.

"On what?" Bundy asked, liking Michelle's style off the bat. She didn't seem the least bit phased by his proposal.

"I need to know, why me?" Michelle looked Bundy in the eye the whole time, a feat some of the most hardened thugs had a problem doing.

"Cause I'm a risk taker, and I've been digging your style from the moment you gave me the once over at the door. Besides, I've got nothing to lose. I can kill two birds with one stone. Tina ain't got four grand to pay me back anyway, and it's you I'm trying to get wit."

"You don't even know me Bundy, so I know you're just trying to beat me in the head and get in the panties."

"True. But I'm trying to beat up the puss and get into the panties. We might as well get this thing right," he smiled, leaning in and whispering "You wanna know a secret?"

"What?" Michelle couldn't help but smile. She had to admit, Bundy's little game of cat and mouse was arousing her.

"I wanna use you to slut Tina out. You know, have her lick your juices off my dick, and eat you out, and any other degrading shit I can think of. You should be wit' it Ma, 'cause how much could she think of you if she even brought my proposition to you." A few seconds passed before Michelle responded.

"Say no more. I'll be right back. Make yourself comfortable, 'cause if we 'bout to get the jump off jumping, we finna do it up right!" Michelle quickly disappeared into the living room.

"What, happened?" Tina asked.

"C'mon. Come to my bedroom." Inside Michelle's bedroom, she threw Tina one of the outfits she wore at the club. "Don't make this a habit Tina. I'ma do this 'cause I see big man ain't playing." She was trying to make Tina more nervous than she already was. "Just, do what he says 'cause I ain't trying to be fucking this horse dick nigga for nothing." By Michelle's statement, *Tina thought Bundy had flashed her the goods. She didn't know it was simply wishful thinking on her roommate's part.*

By the time the two girls entered the room, Bundy had taken the strongest Viagra pill on the market. He'd never used them before, but his mission was to stretch Tina open to the point her vagina had no grippers left. When he saw what the two were wearing, he almost thought his four grand was well spent. *Not quite,* he thought, as he peeped the stretch marks on Tina's stomach from her daughter Brianna's birth.

Michelle's body was tight and taut from all the years of exercising on the stripper pole. She wore a red lace bra and panty set. The part of her outfit that caught Bundy's attention, was the six inch 'fuck me' heels adorned with a lace strap that tied up to her calves and ended in a bow. Tina had on the same outfit, but hers was black. Michelle's feet were also much smaller, so Tina had to pull a pair of pumps out of her own closet.

"C'mere Michelle." Bundy patted his thigh and motioned for Michelle to sit on his lap. The two of them started making out while Tina watched undecided on what to do. Bundy whispered in Michelle's ear, and the next thing Tina knew, Michelle was barking orders at her.

"Bitch, what you standing around looking all stupid for?" Michelle stuck her foot out and yelled, "You see that pedicure? Suck the shine off that motherfucker!" Tina looked at Bundy, who had a look on his face that suggested she do as told. She dropped to her knees and began sucking on Michelle's big toe.

"Suck it like a dick, bitch!" Bundy laughed, seeing that Michelle was adlibbing. He laid Michelle on the bed, and while upside down, began sucking on her bottom lip. Bundy started massaging Michelle's handful of breasts, kneading them slowly, as he pinched her nipples. It caused her to make a hissing sound. "Damn, you getting me wet."

Bundy looked down and saw Tina bobbing her head up and down on her roommate's big toe. "You heard her ho. The pussy's wet, so start sucking it!" Tina had never been with a woman before, and even if she'd wanted to, it wouldn't have been in such a degrading fashion. Michelle took advantage of the moment and ground her sex all in and around Tina's face. She could have given Tina a break, but got too caught up in the moment to care. That's when Bundy flipped Michelle over into the doggy style position.

"Eat that ass, Tina!" He looked Michelle in the eye. "If you don't feel that bum bitch's tongue tickling your asshole, you let Daddy know Ma." Michelle cocked her ass letting Tina know she intended on holding her to Bundy's orders.

"Yes Daddy, you muh'fucking right I will!" She moaned through half closed eyes.

Bundy made Tina spend a little over twenty minutes on Michelle, before entering her in the doggy style position. As he long stroked Michelle, he called Tina to his side. Tina had a blank expression on her face as if she couldn't wait for their session to end. Bundy had done so many years up north looking at magazines such as Buttman, he was practically desensitized to vulgar sex acts. He continued to abuse Tina in every way he could think of.

"Make yourself useful and get back there and suck my nuts." Bundy stuck his thumb in Michelle's ass, while Tina sucked on his nuts. Out of spite, he shifted his torso so that her tongue slipped towards his ass. Tina damn near gagged as she tried to back away, but Bundy stopped her. "Uh uh bitch. Finish what you started." Tina's eyes started to water as she allowed Bundy's violation to continue.

By now, he was all up in Michelle who was writhing in pleasure as he groaned. "Damn this some good shit here. Now this is what pussy 'posed ta feel like umph!" Bundy gripped a handful of Michelle's ass, and slid his thumb even further, as he felt himself about to cum.

"C'mere Bitch!" Tina came to him, and Bundy stuck his dick in her mouth and started cumming. "You filthy garbage mouth whore!" Bundy started snickering, thinking to himself how much he sounded like the white boys in the porno flicks. "Suck the pussy off that dick and swallow my babies." Tina did as told while Bundy continued to taunt her. "That's what clean pussy taste like. Savor it, 'cause you'll never taste it licking your fingers after you diddle yourself, stank bitch!" Bundy spit in her face and spun her around.

"Don't turn your ugly ass around, because your face'll deflate the hardest dicks, and I ain't done with you yet." Tina stuck her ass in the air, moving her vagina towards the head of Bundy's massive erection. The behemoth brawler started shaking his head. "Nah ho. Your stank snatch ain't worthy of this dick. Spread your ass!"

Tina had done anal sex before, but most of her lovers weren't out for revenge, so she tried to appeal to Bundy's merciful side. "Bundy, please..." Bundy smacked her ass so hard; Tina bucked forward and banged her head on the headboard.

"I ain't trying to hear that shit. Shut the fuck up!" Michelle even started to get nervous of his aggression. Bundy forcefully rammed what Michelle estimated to be at least twelve inches of manhood into her tight rectum, snarling, "You better not fucking move!" The scene was as close as Bundy could come to having permission to rape Tina, Michelle thought. She wasn't sure she wanted to continue being a part of the gruesome scene.

"Yeah bitch! It smells better than your pussy in here." Bundy was pounding Tina so hard; she was having trouble catching her breath. Bundy felt a tear on her insides and stroked even harder, and that's when Tina started screaming. Bundy held her firmly by the waist so she couldn't escape his embrace, growling. "Smother her mouth wit' the pussy!"

Michelle was reluctant to oblige, scared that Bundy was about to kill the girl. "Bundy, I think she's had enough. I ain't agree to all this."

Bundy kept stroking like a man possessed. The Viagra

gave him the stamina of a bull. He could no longer feel his penis as he plowed into Tina without an ounce of mercy.

"Bun...dee, if you ..." Bundy tried to pull out and cum on her face, but as soon as Tina felt him release his grip, she bolted for the bathroom gripping her ass cheeks firmly. Bundy started laughing hysterically. At first Michelle thought he'd lost his mind, but when she looked down, she saw a few drops of feces making a trail towards the bathroom door. Tina had locked herself in the bathroom, while Bundy got dressed. When Michelle left the room, Bundy used Tina's pillowcase to wipe his dick before getting dressed.

Bundy left the apartment and jumped in his Range Rover. Michelle came running out of the apartment fully dressed and jumped in the truck with Bundy. "I'm coming with you. I think she wouldn't mind a lil' time to herself." Bundy was laughing, but Michelle wasn't. She didn't know how to feel about what she'd just witnessed.

Chapter9

Future Plans!

One week later...

"That was some flight, huh Precious?" The woman asking the question was Precious' boss Misha Garner. Precious and Misha had just returned from a five day seminar on Criminal Justice, and both were suffering from a bad case of jetlag.

"You're telling the truth Misha. I can't wait to get home and take a nice hot bath."

"Well I appreciated the company. Take a few days off,

because I'll be doing the same. We'll meet up in the office on Wednesday." Misha headed towards the long term parking area of the airport, while Precious hailed a cab.

The ride from LaGuardia Airport to Union Turnpike was a short one. It took the cab no more than fifteen minutes to get Precious home. She paid the cab and stopped when she saw the Platinum Range Rover in the driveway. It didn't surprise Precious at all that Bryce would purchase such a vehicle so soon after coming home in addition to acquiring the Dodge Charger, but the navy blue BMW 5 series was overkill.

"I know this fool didn't up and buy himself two cars," she mumbled. It was close to midnight and Precious wasn't in the mood to try and pry the truth out of Bryce. It wasn't until she got up close to the car that she realized that the car had to belong to a female.

It had tan seats with sky blue piping on the interior. From the rear view mirror hung a pair of sky blue baby Jordan's and a matching tree air freshener. Along the side of the car was a detailed pinstripe with the word 'Babygirl' airbrushed at the end near the gas tank.

"Oh no this nigga didn't go and sneak some bitch up in our bed." Precious marched her way up the steps and burst into the living room ready to lay hands, feet, and toenails to Bryce and whatever slut he had all up in their house. As soon as her eyes settled on the sight before her, she was frozen in her tracks.

"Bryce, what is going on?" Bundy was on the couch sleeping when the sound of his woman's voice woke him out of his weed induced slumber.

"Hey babe. You like?" He was referring to the fully refurnished townhouse. Every single item in their home had been replaced with the newest and latest models. All the appliances from the TV, Stereo and DVD player, down to the refrigerator and stove, were upgraded. A home entertainment system outfitted with Charter Digital and an eighty inch plasma screen stared back at Precious as she stood with her mouth open.

Bryce walked up to her and kissed her full on the mouth before walking her to their new kitchen. "I wanted to surprise you." Bryce beamed with pride as Precious ran her hand across the stainless steel stove top and marble island.

"It's beautiful Bryce, but..."

"But what babe?"

"But where did it all come from? I mean the money. It must have cost you a fortune to do all of this."

"I'm gonna get to that later." Bryce raised his right

hand, swearing. "This time I'm going to tell the straight up truth. I'm thru wit' bullshitting you babygirl." Bryce smiled as he saw Precious' eyes grow wild. For a minute, he thought he'd said something wrong. In all actuality, he'd said just the right thing.

"Babygirl." Precious mumbled, as it finally hit her, "Oh my God, Bryce! Did you buy that car for me?" Precious ran to the window while Bryce stood behind her cheesing. She jumped into Bryce's arms as he spun her around. When he put her down he placed a soft kiss on her forehead, whispering, "Nothing's too good for my baby girl." Bryce touched her face, and Precious noticed the Rolex watch on his wrist, but said nothing. She figured she'd wait since he already swore to tell her everything that was going on.

He walked Precious to their dining room where he had a candlelight dinner waiting for the two of them. They dined on lamb chops, wine, and a cheesecake from Junior's, that waited to be devoured after the main course. It was then that Bryce decided to finally keep it real with Precious... sort of.

"I've been doing a lot of thinking lately babe." Precious could see that Bryce was nervous about whatever it was he was trying to say. She patiently waited for him to get his thoughts together. "I'm starting to realize I've been running these streets in circles, and at the same time, putting my freedom at risk. The streets are like an addiction babe." Precious was wondering what he was getting at. "The same addiction that had me doing all types of armed robberies and home invasions." As his words sunk into Precious' mental, he added, "All the vics were drug dealers," as if it made his admission more acceptable.

Precious wasn't surprised at the act, but the fact that Bryce would admit it had her skeptical. "Why come clean with me now, Bryce?"

He got on one knee and pulled out the Cartier ring box tucked in his pocket. "Because, if I'm hoping to spend the rest of my life with you, then I need to start off by being totally honest with you. I'm trying to wipe the slate clean and start fresh."

Precious could hardly contain her excitement. "Oh my God, Bryce. Are you...?"

"Precious, will you marry...?"

"Yes! Yes! Yes!" She smothered him with kisses. He slipped the ring on her finger as he took in her succulent lips. They rolled around on the floor until Bryce found his way underneath her skirt. Precious tugged at Bryce's belt. He felt her smile against his lips and fondled her through her blouse. Before the two knew it, they were sexing each other on the dining room floor. Bryce's massive hand damn near swallowed up Precious' B cup, as he stroked his thumb across her nipples causing them to grow erect.

"Mmm! Oh man Bryce, I thought..."

"Shhh!" Bryce put a finger to her lips silencing her, as his penis found its way towards her moist entrance. After a few strokes, Bryce was pumping away; for the first time in a while, Precious humped back with passion. Twenty minutes later, they'd still been at it, and had taken their lovemaking session to the bedroom. Precious took her fiancé's penis and put it in her mouth, slowly using her lips to suction the head of his shaft, while making slurping sounds. Her tongue traced the underside of his tip as she gently massaged his balls. Since Precious only came when on top, she waited until her man was so hard the skin on his penis glowed. It was then that she mounted him and rode herself to an intense orgasm. "Um hmm, umm hmm, ooh! I came." She fell into Bryce's arms as the two of them lay exhausted in a state of bliss.

Five minutes into them resting, Precious glanced at the nightstand and saw that Bryce had left her another fifteen grand. It was becoming the magic number, Precious thought, wondering why he kept giving the same amount.

At the moment, she was feeling too good to question Bryce. She thought of the fact that he never did say he was going to end the robberies.

"You sleep?" she asked Bryce, but thought, *don't mess this day up. Remember it just like it is now...perfect.*

"What's up?"

Instead, Precious took her own advice and changed the subject. "Bryce, I appreciate your honesty. I was just wondering." She turned and looked him in the eye. "You wanna just leave here? We can relocate, you know? Just start over."

"Nah, babe. I like it here. New York is where all the action is. All the opportunity is in our hometown. Besides, I ain't feeling them 'bama' niggers." Just that quick, Bryce had deflated Precious' whole evening.

"Who's next?"

Most of the parolee's looked at one another as if they felt sorry for whatever poor bastard had P.O. Williams as their P.O. She scanned the room as her eyes took in the well dressed man rising to enter her office. It wasn't until the ex-con turned in her direction that she realized it was

Bundy.

"Mr. Johnson?"

Bundy's smile confirmed that her assessment was indeed correct. As hard as she tried, P.O. Williams could not hide the fact that she was impressed with his choice of attire. Bundy, realized just how much of an impression a suit made on society. Throughout the entire morning, every woman whose path he crossed nodded his way, or gave him a smile. Bundy even found himself opening doors for the opposite sex, and returning their positive energy.

"Good morning." Bundy gave her a firm handshake, which impressed her. She was a bit of a feminist, and did not like when men treated her with kid gloves. Bundy's firm handshake was taken as a sign that he saw her as an equal. Even if it was done under duress, she appreciated the effort on his part.

"Have a seat, Mr. Johnson." As usual, Ms. Williams showed a no nonsense demeanor.

"I think I'm supposed to give you this." Bundy handed her a pay stub.

Again, Ms. Williams was impressed. "Hmm, you're two-for-one this morning, Mr. Johnson. A job and a change of wardrobe do wonders." She pulled out her pen and began to jot down notes. "Wonders like a curfew extension, and changing your report date to once a month," she smiled, knowing Bundy would appreciate her leniency.

He bolted out of her office like a bat out of hell. The whole time Bundy was thinking about Money's advice to him and how it had gotten his P.O. to finally give him some leeway. *Money, nigga you's a genius.* Bundy planned on making the suits a part of his monthly reporting ritual. As far as he was concerned, Money had a formula, so he followed his homie's lead. Rushing home to change his clothes and check on the block.

Once Bundy got home, he checked himself in the mirror. He was decked out in a pair of Dolce & Gabbana denims in an ice blue color, and his trademark construction Timbs. An 'Affliction' thermal with old English letters two shades lighter than the boots on his feet. The burgundy trim on the letters brought out the platinum cross on his neck. Bundy twisted his neck to the side, loving how the heavy metal swung to and fro, letting it be known that the weight on his chain was proper. To top off his autumn attire, he threw on a two tone North

Face vest in red and black, and a red Dolce & Gabbana skully. He checked the time on his Rolex, and noticed his cell phone was vibrating.

"Talk!" He barked into the phone.

"Don't you want to know who you're talking to first?" Michelle asked.

"I don't know. It depends."

"On what?"

"If you look as good as you sound."

Michelle laughed. It was a deep throaty laugh, one belonging to a woman, a grown woman. "I have nothing to do today Bundy. You feel like coming through and scooping a sister up?"

"Give me about twenty minutes."

"Say no more." And just that quick, the phone went dead.

When Bundy pulled up to the front of the crib, Michelle was already out front waiting on him. This was a good thing, because Bundy wasn't trying to be around Tina for a second longer than necessary. Michelle's appearance threw the big guy for a loop. Michelle was in full tomboy mode when she got in Bundy's Range Rover. She had on an oversized grey hooded sweat suit, and a pair of white on white Nike 'Uptowns.'

"Where to?" Michelle asked, flashing her pearly whites.

"I gotta stop on Murdock. That's okay witchu?"

Michelle shrugged her shoulders. "I'm down wit' whatever playboy."

Bundy was digging her style off the bat. At that moment, Tina stepped on the porch grilling Bundy as if to say, 'You ain't shit!'

"You bum ass bitch. Get a diaper!" he yelled as they made their way to the spot on Murdock Avenue.

Michelle nudged him. "Leave her alone Bundy, I think she's had enough humiliation for the year." Michelle was trying her best not to laugh. As Bundy drove, he tried to roll the blunt in his lap. Michelle saw the trouble he was having and offered him her assistance. "Lemme get that for you." She expertly sealed the Dutch Master cigar in one deft motion. She lit it, and took the first drag, before placing it between Bundy's lips.

"I could get used to having a chick like you around," he smirked.

Ever since Yak had gotten shot, O had taken over all the activities on Murdock. When he pulled up, the workers were on their usual grind. Bundy didn't have the patience for hustling. Robberies of the caliber he was used to were far and few between, so he utilized the block's daily profits to supplement his extravagant spending habits.

"Where the fuck you been all day? I been ringing your phone off the hook, nigga!"

"What?"

"What?" Bundy playfully threw a jab at O. "Who you talking to like that lil' man?" O dipped the jab, and threw two taps to his midsection, pretending not to notice the rock hard abs the big man possessed. After a minute of horse playing, O got down to business.

"Yo, we got a problem."

"I'm listening."

"Lonnie and 'em is fucking up the work. Shit ain't coming back like it should."

"What's up, the bitch too high to get it right or sum'thin?"

O shrugged. "I think she tapping us, 'cause the shit came up short. But I be watching the broad and I don't see where she could be getting over. I'm watching her during the whole process."

"Let's go upstairs. I don't like being out here on Front Street."

Michelle had heard the whole conversation, but said nothing as she followed the two men up to the spot. As they entered the spot, Lonnie and the rest of the addicts in the house got quiet at the sight of Bundy. Michelle gave them all the once over, as she walked up on Lonnie and glanced at her shirt.

"Can I help you?"

Michelle took off her fitted New Era baseball cap and smiled at Lonnie. "Nah, I'm good!"

"Yo Lonnie, what's this I'm hearing 'bout the work not cooking up right?"

Lonnie shrugged her shoulders, shooting game off the top of her dome. "That's what I'm saying Bundy. You know I always did right by you and Yak. I think ya'll need to go see ya'll connect or sum'thin, 'cause the shit ain't coming back right."

Michelle walked over to Bundy and whispered something in his ear. The sight caused Lonnie's eyes to turn to slits, as a wicked grin creased the corners of Bundy's lips.

"How much we got left?" Bundy asked.

Lonnie walked towards the kitchen, extremely sure of herself. She mumbled, "C'mere. Let me show you." Bundy and his crew could hear the shuffle of her cheap slippers across the wooden floor as she got to the setup on the side of the stove. Lonnie stretched her palms right side up as she waved towards the Pyrex pot and other utensils.

"There you go!" rolling her eyes at Michelle as she did a double take.

"Cook it up in front of me Lonnie." Bundy glanced at Michelle, adding, "I wanna see for myself 'fore I go accusing my connect of some off the wall shit. Ya feel me?"

"Humph," Lonnie huffed, knowing Bundy was being politically correct, but suspected her of scamming them. With confidence, and the expertise only an avid user or veteran cook could possess, Lonnie chefed up the cocaine on a skillet until it became a pasty substance. When she was done, she did a curtsey, and with pride announced, "Voila! All done, big boy."

Lonnie started strutting around the apartment, showing her ass. She clucked around like a proud peacock popping shit. Meanwhile, Bundy and Michelle seemed to be having an intense conversation out of her earshot. "I done cooked up pies for some of the biggest ballers in the game Bundy. If I tell you the work ain't correct, then believe me, the shit ain't right!" Lonnie continued her tirade on deaf ears, as O, Bundy, and Michelle waltzed over to the kitchen and inspected the scene.

"I ain't gonna lie. My gut tells me the bitch is pulling some bullshit, but I can't figure out what. I watch the broad like a hawk and get the same results every time." Bundy could sense O's frustration. He wanted to prove that he could run as tight a ship as Yak, but felt as if Lonnie was pulling the wool over his eyes in a way that Yak would have foreseen. It made him feel as if she was fucking up his chances of moving up in the ranks.

"I don't really know shit 'bout this drug shit O." "What could the bitch be doing? Is the scale off? Is it cut wit' some shit that's dissolving the coke?" Bundy had a stupefied look on his face, as he pointed out the obvious. "I mean it ain't like we can complain when we robbed muh'fuckers fa' the shit."

Michelle took in the whole scene with a smirk on her face. Lonnie was truly showing out, while the two men tried desperately to figure out why their product wasn't coming back like it was two days prior. "You think she tapped it wit'..."

Michelle had had enough. She walked up on Lonnie. "Empty your pockets!" This caught Bundy and O's attention. Michelle was leaning forward in a fighting stance.

"Bundy, you need to come get this chick," Lonnie called out to Bundy.

"Why? Just empty your pockets and end all this

confusion for us."

Lonnie turned towards Michelle. "Empty my pockets?"
"What, you think you in jail or sum'thin'?"

Michelle didn't bother with a response; she popped
Lonnie in the jaw and started turning her pockets inside
out. The next thing the men knew, the two women were
scuffling. Michelle handled hers like a pro. She two
pieced Lonnie, and the fight was over before it had begun.
A homemade stem fell out of Lonnie's pocket. When
Michelle saw the pinkish tint of the stem, it suddenly hit
her. She dug inside Lonnie's panties, and pulled out what
appeared to be at least an ounce of crack cocaine.

Bundy grabbed the rock from Michelle, while O lifted
Lonnie by her shirt. Curious, Bundy inspected the crack.
"Why does the shit look like this?" referring to the pinkish
tint. Michelle grabbed a spoon off a nearby table. Pulled
the bottom of Lonnie's shirt out of her jeans and scraped
a spoonful of paste off her shirt. Upon closer inspection,
Bundy and O saw that the pasty substance was their
missing coke.

"Well I'll be damned!" Bundy wanted to laugh, but O
wanted to bash Lonnie's skull in.

Michelle went on to explain. "It's an old trick. When
she cooks, she goes light at first, makes a mess and gets

the work on her shirt. Afterwards, she scrapes it off. The pinkish color is from the red shit. It's a thirsty move that's hardly worth the effort. The bitch is smoking just as much cotton as she is crack, but unfortunately for her, she's dealing with two misers who count every penny, whether they paid for the coke or not."

O was livid. He snatched Lonnie up and put her in the back room with his pitbull, Smokey. Lonnie was shoved into a chair, and knew she was being put on time out. If she even attempted to move out of the chair, Smokey would chew her a new asshole. Lonnie knew from experience that O had been known to leave violators on timeout for days at a time. Since the room had no windows, she knew she was assed out until O remembered she was back there.

When O returned to the kitchen, he overheard Bundy thinking aloud. "Damn, who we finna get to cook this shit up now?"

Michelle took off her sweater, tied her hair in a bun, and stated, "Don't sweat it. I got ya'll." From the moment she went to work in the kitchen, O could tell she knew what she was doing.

"Your knuckle game was shocking enough, but I would've never guessed there was a hustler underneath the heels and short skirts."

Michelle playfully flipped him the bird, as she broke down the origin of her coke-linary skills. "I used to fuck with this cat named Manny, God bless him from Laurelton. He ran a coke cab, for these dudes called 'The Black Rose Family.' He taught me everything I know, so know that you're in good hands gentlemen."

"Shit, 'Chelle, you got a sister? 'Cause if so, if she's anything like you, I'm wife-ing the bitch!"

Michelle laughed. "Just know that I want in, nigga. I'm sick of shaking my ass for dollars. A bitch is looking for her next come up. I've got future plans Cat-daddy!"

Chapter 10
All Bets Are Off!

*M*ost people would have pulled up to the front of their workplace with pride if they were pushing a brand new BMW coupe. The parking lot in front of Solomon, Berry, and Myers was reserved for employees only, but Precious took the scenic route to the underground parking complex across the street from the courthouse. The last thing she wanted was Loretta noticing the extravagant purchase. She glanced at the ring on her finger, and for a brief moment, thought about taking it off.

Now that things appeared to be looking up for Precious, she regretted telling Loretta all of her and Bryce's personal business. *Shoot. Actually, I can't remember if I told her or if she got me to tell her.* Thinking to herself how persistent Loretta could be when she sensed stress in one of her girlfriends. During Bryce's incarceration, the need to vent her stress practically seeped from Precious' pores. It was Loretta who had become the voice of reason during those times. Now that she wanted to live in blissful ignorance of Bryce's nefarious acts, she feared that Loretta would see straight through her facade and pick up on her doubts and worries.

When she entered the office, Precious was surprised to see Loretta coming out of the elevator adjacent to hers. Just as luck would have it, her girl wasted no time inquiring about her time off. "Precious, how was your weekend girl?"

Precious shrugged, but Loretta had no intention of letting it go at that. To make matters worse, Loretta was also every bit of a morning person, with or without her double latte Espresso. Once inside their cubicles, Precious sat down and placed her hands or her face. She knew she wasn't going to be able to hide her concerns from Loretta.

She was figuring out a way to express herself, when fate started the conversation for her.

"Oh my God! No he didn't!" Loretta looked around the office, catching herself before one of her co-workers noticed her outbreak. Precious wondered what the commotion was about, then noticed that she'd forgotten her ring was on.

"How many carats is that bad boy?" Loretta was practically twisting Precious' arm trying to get a good look at her engagement ring.

"Can I have my hand back Loretta?" Precious managed half a smile.

Loretta let go of her hand, giggling, "Oh, my bad! No wonder you're so tired. Girl, I know that man must have kept you up all night earning that rock." Loretta's joke caused Precious to blush, as she shushed her. "Damn, Precious! What did Bryce do, bust some old rich woman in the head for it?" Loretta was simply being her playful self, but Precious wondered if the statement held merit.

"He has a job doing security, and sometimes the clients are rappers and celebrities who pay a lil' extra to keep their business personal I guess."

"Shoot, ole' Loretta can keep a secret. How can I be down?"

I can't believe I'm sitting here using Bryce's lies on my friend. She wished Loretta would switch subjects, but she was happy for her, and knew that a proposal wasn't something that girlfriends rushed through like an episode on UPN. Knowing Loretta, Precious was sure that Bryce's proposal would be the conversation of the day.

"So, I guess it's safe to say that things are looking up, huh?" Precious smiled, while Loretta continued, "Have you told anybody yet?"

"To be honest Loretta, it's still settling in. I'm trying to digest all of these events, and it's been such a short amount of time. I don't think the reality of it all has soaked into my brain yet." It was the first time during their morning talk that Precious was being totally honest in her choice of words.

"Well, I'm glad things are going good wit' ya'll Precious. Lunch is on me girl; you know I'm not done with you by a long shot."

Precious nodded as she waved Loretta off. By lunchtime she figured half of the firm would be dropping by her desk to congratulate her. *Well, I guess today is going to be a long day Precious.* She was glad that she had parked the BMW nowhere near the office. *One surprise at a time,* she giggled, taking one last look at her ring.

One minute, she wasn't sure how to feel about it all, and the next she was feeling elated by the prospects of what the future held.

"I'm a mess," she uttered, as she prepared for her day of work.

Precious wasn't the only one suffering from a case of conflicted emotions. Bundy was cruising down the B.Q.E, reflecting on Chico's words. Bundy had never taken the time to find out the cause of his addiction to robberies. The rush he felt, combined with his power and control issues were never dealt with during his nearly half decade prison stint.

"He's right," Bundy murmured, to no one in particular. He was referring to Chico's analogy of the carrot on a stick. Bundy had come to the realization that he needed to focus his energy on a legal way to produce the funds that could maintain his extravagant tastes. The problem was, he was damn near broke. Since no real income was coming in and he was spending money as if it was being replaced by a daily profit, he had depleted his funds. Before he knew it, he was making plans for one last jux. To make matters worse, Bundy was superstitious. Many times during his bid, he'd heard the stories from other convicts who stated that their initial offense was supposed to be their last one. Nine out of ten times, it was the very crime that led them to having those infamous silver bracelets slapped on their wrists.

Even subconsciously, Bundy was planning for his own demise. He had already been plotting on a patron at the club known only as Nick. Nick was a very cautious individual who moved in the street like clockwork. Every other night, at the same time, he could be seen in and out of the Player's Lounge. He even regulated his time there, never spending more than two hours at a time before snatching up some brown skinned button nosed cutie to end the night off with. Nick would have seemed like any other player at the Player's Lounge. He wasn't flashy enough to stand out to the average hustler, however, this nonchalant attitude and conservative style was exactly what made the big man single Nick out. By trying not to look like money, Nick gave off the exact air that he was trying to downplay.

The last time he came to the Player's Lounge, Chico treated him like royalty. Bundy started to wonder who he was. Nick had entered the club in true VIP fashion. Pulling up in his Pearl white Mercedes CL600, which had every accessory from the rear view mirrors to the door handles, including chromed out rims. The peanut butter interior matched his construction Timbs to the tee. Bundy was sure the rest of the security team that he now managed due to Gooch's sudden demise was going to turn Nick away based on his dress code; a V-neck Hanes tee-shirt, tan 'Roc-A-Wear' military type cargo pants, and Timbs. Besides his wedding band, he wore a platinum Audemar Piguet watch. The way the bouncers nodded in acknowledgement of Nick, and pulled back the velvet rope for him to enter, spelled it out to Bundy. 'He's the one!'

He justified his last jux by telling himself two things; first, in order to retire, he needed enough cash to invest in something; second, O would be left out in the cold until Yak's return. In reality, he was simply recruiting O as his wingman for the jux since Yak seemed to have fallen back since his near death experience. Bundy had gone as far as to scheme on his approach concerning robbing Nick.

Like everything else Nick did, even his choice of women stayed consistent. He liked his women petite with a brownish honey coated hue, chinky eyes, and a bubbled onion booty. His taste fit Michelle's description to a tee, down to her new Rihanna hairdo.

Bundy turned off at the next exit. He had his mind made up. Nick would be his next vic and Michelle would be the bait.

Almost immediately after Bundy arrived at Murdock, Sosa turned the corner in his BMW and tapped the horn twice waving in his direction. Bundy waved back, thinking, *He seems to be doing alright.*' Bundy had half expected Sosa to eventually get up the nerve to try and take his block back. Ever since his eviction, Sosa seemed to be taking the whole loss in stride. "I guess it's true what they say, you can't keep a real hustler down," Bundy said to himself, as he silently saluted Sosa for staying on his grind despite his circumstances.

When he entered the spot, Michelle was bagging up the work while O sat reading a copy of Hip-Hop Weekly. Bundy took a seat, making himself comfortable. O looked up. "Can you believe this shit? Remy Ma blows trial, while R. Kelly gets acquitted. Unfucking-believable!"

Michelle was the one who had gotten O hooked on the weekly tabloid. She laughed the same sexy laugh that turned Bundy on. "Shit, that's how you do that shit! Kellz stalled that trial so long, by the time they put that broad on the witness stand, she was a grown woman."

"I feel bad for Remy, but on the real, whenever the courts rush yo' case like they did hers, more than likely they 'bout to railroad your ass."

O read a little further, then started bugging. "Yo 'Chelle, it says here that the nigga Papoose was wildin' in the court on the bailiffs. That's what's up!" Bundy just watched the two of them go back and forth.

"They're a good look. That's what I need, a ride or die nigga! At least ole' girl can get a few trailers. That shit makes the bid a lil' bit easier." She looked up at Bundy and stared him dead in the eye, adding, "You know, knowing you can get a bit of loving every now, and then."

Bundy shook his head. "Will you look at you two? Ya'll sound like some real groupies right now." Bundy snatched the tabloid from O and started thumbing through it. "Chris Brown and Ciara? What's that about?"

"Lemme find out we ain't the only groupies," Michelle laughed. Bundy and O couldn't help but to join in the laughter.

All of a sudden, a shot rang out, followed by several others. The glass shattered, causing O to hit the floor and pull out the Tech-9 stashed underneath the sofa cushion. Bundy already had his Desert Eagle out, and was surprised to see Michelle flip behind the couch and come up with a Glock 40 aimed at the door.

I think I'm falling in love wit' this bitch, O thought, as Michelle winked at Bundy.

"You first big fella." She nodded towards the door, as Bundy leapt forward as if he was possessed. He had no idea how bloodthirsty he'd become since his time in prison had his gun game on hiatus. It had been a long time since Bundy found himself drawing his pistol on even terms. He soon discovered it was just like riding a bike. No matter how long it's been, you never forget.

"Michelle! Shoot out the window. O, come on!" The two men burst out the back door. Michelle's gunfire caused the intruders to concentrate on the upstairs window. Bundy and O were able to creep up on the attackers from the rear, and wound two of them on sight. Bundy walked over to one guy who was squirming and writhing from the pain, peeped the vest he had on, and shot him in the center of his forehead. O saw two young boys hiding behind a Volkswagen Passat, and let off the Tech in succession to keep them at bay. O noticed the boys cowering, and realized that whoever they were, they realized they'd bitten off more beef than they could chew. One of the boys looked to be of Spanish decent, which made O think instantly of Fernando.

"Muh'fuckers!" He gave chase, surprised to see one of the teens had gone as far as dropping his gun. Bundy scooped the gun up and tucked it in his waist as he tried to catch up to O. The two men never saw the man in the black hoodie creeping up the stairs to the spot. Luckily, Michelle did. She opened the door to the room that held O's pitbull Smokey, and was immediately hit in the nostrils by the foul stench of urine and feces.

"Damn Smokey," Michelle whispered, thinking that O had neglected to walk his beloved pooch. It wasn't until Lonnie bolted past her, that Michelle smelled the stench coming off her.

"Lonnie, no!" It came out as a hoarse whisper. Before Michelle could stop her, Lonnie had snatched the door open and was cut down by gunfire from the hooded assailant at the door. Lonnie's mistake became Michelle's good fortune as she pumped four bullets into the gunman and released Smokey on him. Corpse or not, Smokey tore into him, until Michelle snatched him by the leash, and the two bolted out the door.

For a brief second, she looked around for Bundy and O. The incoming police sirens forced her to make tracks in the opposite direction. A block away, she tossed the gun inside a neighbors flower pot, stripped off her Black Hand Entertainment hoodie, and pretended to be taking Smokey for his morning walk.

"Damn! Bundy, O, where the fuck ya'll at?" Not even five minutes passed before Michelle's phone started to chime. It was Bundy.

"Where you at?" Him and O were sitting adjacent to the rock on Farmers and 109, where Bundy had Gooch meet him before.

"At a cab stand. But they won't let me ride with Smokey."

"Which one?" After Michelle told him, Bundy told her to hold tight. A few minutes later, the three of them were on the highway heading nowhere fast. O was busy checking Smokey for injuries, while Michelle stared at Bundy, grateful that he was unscathed. Bundy, on the other hand, was calculating how much money they'd just loss. He knew that after this second incident, the police would have one of those makeshift mobile precincts parked on Murdock Avenue 24/7.

"Muh'fuckers done shut down shop!"

The following day had Bundy brooding all morning. Precious had no idea what he was going through, and took his mood change as him having second thoughts concerning his proposal. Bundy sat alone in the living room while Precious was at work. What he didn't realize was that he was extremely institutionalized. Even as a free man, Bundy was conditioned to being in a cell. The living room of his own home had become his cell. He'd actually come to enjoy having time to himself while Precious was away. Anytime he found himself getting close to someone, Bundy would withdraw. He withdrew from Precious, Chico, and pretty much had traumatized Tina for the sake of principle.

The mail slot to the front door flipped open as the mailman dropped off the morning mail. Bundy pretty much just handed Precious money and let her pay the bills, so unlike most adults, he flipped through the stack of letters half interested, that is, until one letter heading in particular caught his interest.

He recognized the heading as the print shop's bold letterhead from Auburn Correctional Facility. When he opened it up, he saw that it was a letter from his old associate Born. Bundy didn't care too much for Born, but tolerated him. According to the prison grapevine, Born's people were some heavy hitters out of Harlem who were top dawgz in the dope game. When Bundy was nearing the end of his sentence, he had given Born his info just in case he found himself with limited options and was inclined to give the heroin hustle a go. Other than that, he 'tried not to deal with Born based on the many rumors circling the yard about his shady character.

He sat on the couch, peeled open the letter, and expected to hear the news that Born was touching down along with the big willie talk of just how much cash was theirs for the taking. Instead, he got the total opposite.

Greetings Comrade!

In case you haven't figured it out by my name and number, its Born giving you a shout out. By the time this scribe reaches you, I hope it finds you in the best of health and good spirits. Your man Al-Boogie couldn't take it anymore, and stabbed the God, U-Majesty over that debt he owed. The

God is forced to wear a colostomy bag and
he pressed charges on Al, so the boy got an
eight flat running wild.

Aw man Boogie that dough wasn't 'bout nothing. Bundy pressed his thumb against his temple. He was feeling the beginning stages of a headache coming on, but continued reading.

> *I know you're probably mumbling to*
> *yourself that it wasn't worth it, but, you know*
> *how it is behind the wall. It's the principle of*
> *the thing, ya know?*

"Nah, I don't know," Bundy answered the letter. The truth of the matter was he knew exactly what Born meant. He had an open date when he knocked U-Majesty on his ass over that same debt. He was too emotional to make the connection. He thought about how much stress his boy Al-Boogie must have been under with a fresh 8 tacked onto his sentence. He continued to read Born's scribe.

Al ain't the only one who fucked up son. I fucked up my shit.

> *With 90 days to go, I done fucked around*
> *and put some boy in the hospital. I had took*
> *a liking to the kid, and next thing I know,*

*I'm spotting the kid while he's curling, and
the boy tries to stab me. Basically, I got a
case pending. The word on the street is, you
doing it big, so I figure it won't hurt to ask.
I need a lawyer son. We thoroughbreds. I'll
plug you in to my fam up in Harlem, so you
can...*

Bundy crumbled up the letter and threw it in the trash.
He knew who the boy was Born was referring to, and
knowing Born's history, could piece the rest together
himself.

Bundy remembered the lanky kid named Light when
he first came on the Auburn tier. Light was from Buffalo
and weighed 120 pounds tops, with rocks in his pockets
and soaking wet. Bundy could tell by the look in his eyes
that Light was scared to death and on his first bid. He had
accidentally killed one of his friends while cleaning his
father's gun. His father, an ex-Marine, had concocted a
story about teaching Light gun safety in preparation for
Military school.

Since the D.A. couldn't prove otherwise, and Light had no criminal history, she agreed to offer Light a plea bargain in the form of an eight year sentence. With good behavior, Light could see the streets in six and a half years, so his Pops made him jump on the plea.

Born was a known 'Booty-Bandit' throughout the state. He was never officially caught in the act. Whenever one of Born's allies caught him fraternizing with one of the prison gumps, he would always make up some lame excuse about them being a family member he couldn't just turn his back on. After a while, the lame excuse grew tired, and most of the God bodies ostracized him. The only reason Born didn't suffer at the hands of a universal beat down was because of the fact that, despite his sexual preference, the God got busy.

Prison had changed so much over the years that the State was giving out new bids for assaults that landed no more than a short term keep lock back in the days. Booty-bandits like Born had to switch to soft shoe tactics. Hoping their prey was weak enough to let their own fears cause them to give in to the demands of undercover homo thugs like Born. Even a weaker inmate putting up half a fight would get the support of the majority of straight men who didn't condone such behavior. Contrary to popular belief, most men in prison simply relied on Ms. Palm and her five daughters, before they'd disgrace themselves.

Bundy remembered that plenty of times he'd seen Born spot the kid Light from the rear when he curled weights, as opposed to the common method of face-to-face. He figured one of the cons must have put Light on, and forced the youth to remedy the situation before it was too late. Bundy surmised that Light probably went into the battle half heartedly. Born being the violent veteran he was, beat the kid half to death.

Bundy had no intention on helping out such a man. He did however, plan on doing whatever he could to help his man Al-Boogie's situation. "That faggot ass nigga Born can rot on his cot though," Bundy uttered. He was stressed out, so he did the only thing that seemed to calm his nerves. He jumped in his truck, lit a blunt, and made his way to Jamaica Avenue to go shopping.

Just the sight of Jamaica Avenue was enough to put a smile on the big fella's face. The traffic of apple bottomed cuties had given him his swagger back in an instant. He copped a pair of Jordan XX3's in black along with a black Jordan warmup suit, and matching headband. He was about to send Al-Boogie a pair, then realized he was more than likely unable to receive packages at the moment.

Instead, he got a $300 dollar money order, and put a short note on the back of the receipt before mailing it off to him. As he returned to the parking area above the Coliseum to retrieve his truck, he saw the street vendor Massamba on 164th Street selling the hottest and latest Urban Fiction novels in the game. Bundy was particular on which ones he read. As a criminal, he felt a lot of the stories were too over the top and were more than likely written by some college student who penned what he or she thought men of his ilk wanted to read; a ghetto fairytale.

He looked for the authors who had lived the life, but were smart enough to turn their bad experiences into cautionary tales for the youth who thought they now had the formula to do the wrong thing the right way. Novels that were confessions of a thug seeking redemption and trying to give back while providing for their family. He copped 'Miz's Bishop' as well as the sequel 'The Bulldog Crew,' Randy Kearse's, 'Changing Your Game Plan', and 'Blueprints of Time' by DeWright Johnson Jr.

"If you buy six books, I'll give 'em to you for forty-five dollars," Massamba stated. Bundy grabbed two more books, 'Family Comes First' Parts I & 2, by Tracy Thomas.

Bundy read the back of one of the books, and snickered, "'The Black Rose Family,' huh? This nigga gets a whole team of real killers, and all I can find is four, and one of 'em is a chick. Shit, I wish real life was as glamorous as these books and films."

Massamba simply summed his cynicism up as bad humor as Bundy continued down the street.

Later that night...

"Damn! Where the fuck is this dude? He picked a hell of a time to be running late." Chico was furious with Bundy but kept his composure. He was in the process of trying to convince DJ Deuce that he'd found Gooch's replacement. Chico had already given Bundy the job as head of security, but was now in the midst of pitching the big man for Gooch's side job.

The side job involved prepping the Player's Lounge patrons' vehicles for the transport of cocaine. Unbeknown to most, Chico's club was a depot for a third of the drugs in the tri-state area. The same way Gooch had prepped 'Sosa BMW months prior, was the same method a dozen other dealers used. Gooch was also responsible for picking up the cash for the drugs, being that Chico never allowed that part of the transaction to go down at the lounge. It was how Gooch had gotten involved with Red in the first place. Red had figured Gooch to be trustworthy since Chico felt comfortable enough to send him to pick up his cash.

Chico had kept his illegal activities a secret from Bundy. Based on the fact that his penchant for robberies conflicted with his own hustling. Now, Chico found himself going against his better judgment, hoping that in Bundy's quest for income, he would push aside the robberies for a hustle that was a bit more consistent.

"Listen, I gotta be somewhere. Sit on this plan of yours before you jump out the window. We need a guy who is reliable." Deuce scanned the parking lot, before adding, "And being late is not a good first impression. Ya feel me?" Chico nodded. After all, Deuce was the boss.

Lately, Bundy and Chico had been growing distant. Where Chico's distance was to give his homeboy time to think, Bundy's withdrawal was based partly on confusion. He finally showed up to work his shift at the Player's Lounge, totally disregarding the club's strict dress code. All members of the security squad were expected to at least wear the blazers supplied by the club. Bundy arrived in the same Jordan outfit he'd copped on the Ave. hours earlier. By the look on Chico's face, Bundy knew he was pissed off, but was in no mood to explain himself.

"Yo, where you been? You're over an hour late."

"Please Chico, not now."

"Not now?"

"Yeah, I said not now!"

Chico backed off knowing that Bundy didn't possess the characteristics required for the job of transporting. *I don't know what the fuck I was thinking,* Chico thought. "You know what, cool. Not now it is." He spun on his heels leaving Bundy to believe he'd won the war.

Bundy spent most of the night sulking in a far off corner in the back of the Player's lounge, leaving all of his duties to the rest of the security team. It wasn't until three in the morning that his assistance was finally needed. One of the customers began getting unruly, and Jock, one of the bouncers, brought the scene to Bundy's attention.

"Bundy, we've got a problem with this dude, and he ain't trying to work wit' us. What should we do?" When Bundy looked towards the scene, the patron had just pushed one of the doormen.

"Get yo' muh'fucking hands off a me nigga!" He put his hands in the bouncers face, snarling, "Touch me again, and I will clap yo' faggot ass!" He reached under his shirt like he was strapped, causing Bundy to calmly walk over to the man. He knew Chico had strict rules regarding the use of force in such situations. At all costs aggression was to be avoided.

"What's the problem here?" The patron took two steps back when he saw Bundy, and barked on him.

"Mind yo' motherfucking business chump! This is between..." That was all he managed to get out before Bundy began laying hands on him. The first blow landed ole' boy dead on his ass. Bundy scooped him up and slammed him on top of one of the tables. He didn't even let the man go. He lifted him off his feet a second time and flung him against the wall. All of the wind was knocked out of him, as Bundy kicked the front door to the club open, and flung the rowdy patron out of the lounge as if he was a ragdoll. Bundy returned to his table as if nothing had happened and continued to sip on his drink.

He caught sight of one of the waitresses and waved her over. "Cat, bring, me another round of Me'nage." Bundy didn't even notice how uneasy Catalina was. They had a bit of a rapport. When she saw his bad side, Catalina felt as if she didn't really know the gentle giant she'd come to favor.

About an hour passed, and the whole time Chico

avoided Bundy like the flu. Even his security team left him to wallow in whatever issues he had going on. Chico was debating whether or not to give him the night off, when circumstances wound up making the choice for him. One of the bouncers began smiling from ear to ear as he pulled aside the velvet rope for none other than Nick.

Damn! Bundy thought, realizing he hadn't even had time to set up his plan with Michelle. He pulled out his cell phone figuring he could get her on the line and update her on his scheme once she got to the club. He waited for a few rings, but wound up getting her voicemail. Nick waltzed right past Bundy, and when he peeped the rose gold Patek Phillipe watch on his wrist, he'd convinced himself that he couldn't pass up his chance for a come up at Nick's expense. He bolted out of his seat, and immediately began searching for Chico.

The first person he ran into was Catalina. "Cat, where's Chico?"

"I think I saw him, heading to his office..." Bundy bolted before she could finish her sentence. When, he got to Chico's office, he gave the door three hard knocks, before Chico answered.

"Come in."

Bundy stuck his head in the door. "Yo Chico, I think I

should take the night off. My head ain't right and I don't wanna fuck up any more than I already have."

Thank God, Chico thought. Instead of saying it aloud, he kept his poker face. "Aight, I'll see you tomorrow morning?"

"No doubt!" Bundy grinned a mischievous smile, adding a half interested nod before returning to the rear of the lounge to scope out Nick's movements.

Nick pretty much kept to himself most of the night, and Bundy noticed that none of the women in the club seemed to match the description of Nick's preference. "Damn 'Chelle, where the fuck you at when I need you," he murmured. Finally, Nick made his way to the exit, with Bundy hot on his heels. Lucky for Bundy, the rest of the security team thought he was escorting Nick on the hush, because they usually made sure Nick made it to his car alright. Bundy was the only one who seemed unaware of Nick's connection to the Player's Lounge.

Once outside, Nick put the key to his whip in the door, and that's when he felt the sharp blow to the back of his ear causing everything to go black. Bundy stuffed the now hogtied Nick into the rear cargo space of his Range Rover, and pulled off dialing O.

"Yo, who the fuck is calling me at this hour?" O was

still in the process of trying to get his faculties in order. He wiped the sleep out of his eyes, as Bundy replied, "Nigga if you don't want in on this paper, I'll call you back when you're up, and you can watch me spend it." The prospect of easy money snapped O out of his slumber.

"I'm up, I'm up! What's up?"

"Meet me across the street from the bicycle shop on the Ave. O already had one leg in his jeans. "Nigga, you got forty-five minutes!"

Chapter 11

Keep Ya Friends Close.

The next morning...

$\mathcal{B}$undy had never in his life experienced a robbery as easy as Nick. Nick cooperated fully and seemed to only be concerned about not getting hurt. It almost seemed too easy. Nick took them to his stash house and handed over a quarter million dollars in cash. What Bundy didn't know was that the older Nick was a veteran in the street game, and had actually put money aside for just that type of situation. Nick was actually Chico and DJ Deuce's connect.

When Bundy entered Chico's office, he was on the phone. Nick was explaining the events of the night before.

"Let me make sure I understand you correctly Nick." Chico motioned for Bundy to have a seat. He wanted him to hear the conversation he was having with Nick. "They kidnapped you from the parking lot of the club?" Chico had looked over at Bundy who was staring at the ceiling with a smirk on his face. Bundy's attitude towards the whole thing seemed adolescent to Chico. After he hung up the phone, Chico began filling Bundy in on the details of the robbery.

Bundy immediately got defensive. "Okay, but why are you telling me?"

"Why am I telling you? Well, for starters, you're head of my security team. Don't you think this is something you should be aware of?"

Bundy shrugged. It was then that Chico realized, Bundy didn't even view what they had as a friendship.

He realized that Bundy still felt he owed him, and Chico came to the conclusion that he was simply paying off a debt for a mistake that was almost half a decade old.

"Bundy, is there something you need to tell me?"

Bundy had a blank expression on his face, as if he had no idea what Chico was getting at. "Nope." Then he faked as if he'd gotten the picture. "Wait, you think I robbed him? C'mon man, you know me better than that."

"Aight, I just needed to know. If you did we can try and fix it, but if you say you didn't, I'm gonna hold you to your word." Chico reached in his desk and fished out Bundy's paycheck. "After all, we're friends, right?" Chico stared him dead in the eye.

"And you know this man." Bundy mimicked Chris Tucker.

Chico noted that the whole time Bundy never made eye contact with him. He was too busy staring at his paycheck.

"I got some shit to take care of Chico. I'll see you tonight." With that said, Bundy made his way out of the club.

That night, Bundy came to the club thinking about the two hundred grand he had stashed at his crib. He had given O fifty large, since he'd done pretty much next to nothing to receive that. Bundy had to fight to remind himself of the promise he made of this being his last jux. He also made a mental note to begin his quest for his investment opportunity. He thought of a few old homies who were legitimate ballers and figured he'd pick their brain for a legal hustle suited to his taste.

After an hour of daydreaming, Bundy saw Sosa enter the club and nodded in his direction. Although he had a newfound respect for Sosa, to pretend they were still as tight as they used to be seemed too much of a stretch for the big man. So he gave Sosa his space. Bundy sat in the rear of the club, which was becoming his makeshift office as of late. He began thumbing through a car dealership brochure for Bentleys.

"Everything good?"

When Bundy turned to look, he saw Chico over his shoulder peeping the brochure. It was too late to hide it without appearing guiltier than he already did, so he rolled with the punches.

"I'm hanging in there Chico. I was thinking 'bout your carrot on a stick spiel. I decided I'd dedicate this month

towards finding myself a legitimate business to invest in."
Bundy faked a smile.

Chico followed suit, faking one of his own. "You looking to cop?" He pointed at a GT Convertible, but before Bundy could answer, continued, "I didn't know I was paying you that much. You must really be stacking your checks." Chico was gone before he could figure out the hidden meaning of the statement.

Fuck him! Nigga acting all emotional. Bundy slid outside to smoke a blunt. By the time he re-entered the club; he got the shock of his life and started to panic.

"Aw fuck!" He popped an Altoid breath mint at the sight of his Parole Officer making her way into the club with one of her girlfriends in tow. He was trying to figure a way to get the scent of the chronic out of his clothes when he saw her give Chico a big bear hug. The sight made him take in her attire, and that's when he realized she wasn't visiting the club in an official capacity. She had on a formfitting evening gown that showed plenty of cleavage in the front, and a pair of high heeled pumps that showed off her pedicure.

"Damn she cleaned up nice," Bundy mumbled, wondering what to do next. Before he could figure it out, he caught sight of Chico and pulled him to the side. "Yo that was my P.O. You know her?" Chico glanced around but Bundy stopped him. "Don't look. She's the one who just gave you the hug."

"Who, Shawna? Oh shit, she's your P.O.? Man, you could be worse off, but she ain't too hard to win over." Chico laughed, shaking his head.

"Nah, fuck that. I'm out!"

"See you tomorrow," Chico shouted. Lately, he was feeling like the Player's Lounge was better off without Bundy there.

Outside, Bundy went to stick his key in the door of his Range, and saw the brief remnants of a reflection. He spun around reaching behind his back for the .357 snub nose, when he saw it was his P.O. and her partner.

"Yo, you scared the shit outta me Ms. Williams." Bundy faked like he was hiking up his jeans before Shawna caught on to the fact he was carrying a gun.

"Is this you?" she smiled. Bundy could have sworn he saw a hint of admiration in her eyes. Or was that, respect? *Lemme find out she respects a paper chaser.*

"Are you listening to me Mr. Johnson?"

"Huh?" Bundy snapped out of his trance.

"I said are you listening to me?" He'd never seen Shawna Williams smile before. He liked it.

"Oh yeah, that's me. You like it?"

"I'd like to know how you can afford such luxuries. I'm sure Chico is paying you, but not like that."

"What happened was..."

Shawna raised her hand silencing him. "I'm just messing with you Mr. Johnson. If you are doing something illegal on the side, the truth has a way of always coming to the light. Until then, I'll give you the benefit of the doubt."

Shawna and her sidekick returned to the Player's Lounge. Bundy hopped in his truck and made his way out of the parking lot. As he approached the exit, he caught a glimpse of Sosa whispering in Chico's ear in front of the spot. *Sosa sure has been getting around lately,* he thought to himself.

At that moment, he got a call on his cell phone, and when he looked at his caller ID, he saw it was Michelle. *Damn! Now you call. Where was you when I needed you?* Bundy chose to let the call go to voicemail, as he rushed home to give Precious some much needed time.

Precious had a habit of taking late night jogs before turning in to go to sleep. As she rounded the corner to her house, she noticed Bryce's car was parked in the driveway for a change. She thought about trying for a second time to convince him that relocating was their best option. Ever since Bryce had admitted what he was doing in the 'hood, Precious had constant nightmares about her and Bryce being on the receiving end of a home invasion. She couldn't shake the feeling that one of Bryce's former victims would come back to seek revenge on him, or her, just for the sake of not leaving any witnesses.

Precious was a firm believer that what goes around, comes back around.

Meanwhile, Bundy was inside the house having thoughts of his own. He had just come back from revisiting the car lot on Queens Boulevard. He was having second thoughts concerning the hundred grand he'd just dropped on the cherry red Bentley GT Convertible. To make matters worse, he'd spent an extra ten grand to have the convertible top in a matching reddish cloth, so that along with its red interior the Bentley would be 'blooded out.'

After going to the insurance agent on Sutphin Boulevard, he found out that there was more to owning a Bentley than meets the eye. Bundy was informed that although his insurance would cover the damages on another vehicle, more times than not, the other vehicle probably couldn't cover any real damage to his whip.

"I guess that's what they mean when they say a nigga's really ballin'. If you can afford it, you've gotta be able to afford it all the way across the board."

"Bryce, are you talking to yourself?"

When he looked up, he saw Precious standing in front of him drying off with a towel.

"Just thinking out loud."

"Oh, I thought that cell had gone and drove my man crazy." She smiled hoping her joke didn't offend him. She'd noticed he'd been so moody lately, she didn't know when a little humor was appropriate.

When Bryce saw the grey Gap sweat suit Precious was wearing, he asked "Why didn't you wear one of the new suits in your closet?"

"I don't see what the difference is? I'm just going to sweat in them anyway. Besides, I pulled out one and noticed it was a Gucci warm up suit. When I saw the price, I couldn't picture myself sweating it up."

"Aight. Whatever!" Bundy didn't even bother to debate.

"I'm gonna go shower and freshen up."

Bundy gave Precious a half nod. His mind was elsewhere. He was still thinking about the words of his insurance agent, and how he'd invested in nothing tangible out of all his extravagant spending. *More bills equal more juxes*. He scanned his mental rolodex for the men he'd try and focus on for legitimate investments. "Carrot on a stick," he mumbled. Then his mind suddenly went blank.

Chapter 12

The Epiphany!

"You've gotta grow the fuck up B! I don't owe you shit. You're not gonna have me bending over backwards trying to appease you for an almost five year old error in judgment." Bundy was shocked to hear Chico talking to him in such a manner.

Deuce sat on the side of Chico's desk saying nothing. Robbing Nick was bad enough, but Bundy not coming clean and admitting to it had forced Chico's hand. He and Deuce agreed that they couldn't have a person in their spot that they couldn't trust. To add insult to injury, Bundy had pulled into the Player's Lounge parking lot in his brand new Bentley GT Convertible fitted with 22 inch reddish chromed out Asanti rims. Regardless of how disappointed Chico and Deuce were, Bundy had no intentions of handing over the last chunk of change he had. If they wanted Nick's money back, they had to get it in blood.

"You ain't gotta worry 'bout appeasing me homeboy. I'm good!" Bundy saw his guilt trip wasn't working.

"Yeah I'm glad you said that, 'cause you don't work here anymore. At least my conscience can rest easy, knowing I ain't leaving you out in them streets fucked up."

"Yeah, well don't worry 'bout me nigga. I could never sit around and just be fucked up." With that said, Bundy got up from Chico's desk and exited the lounge. Although their views differed, Bundy saw that Chico was as firm in his beliefs as he was when it came to his criminal lifestyle.

"Mr. Johnson!"

Here we go again, thought Bundy. He had to admit that he felt a bit more at ease seeing Ms. Williams in civilian clothes, and knowing her first name. It made him feel as if they were on more even terms. She must have felt the same, because her whole demeanor had switched from no nonsense to courteous.

"Were you out there long?"

"No longer than usual Ms. Williams." Bundy went out of his way to keep it cordial. The last thing he wanted to do was overplay his hand and get too comfortable. His P.O. went through her normal routine, and it wasn't until Bundy handed over his final pay stub from the Player's Lounge that Shawna opened up to him.

"I see Chico and Deuce pay you some pretty decent pennies, huh?"

Bundy shrugged, mumbling, "I do alright. But them boys are the real ones balling." He gave an uncomfortable chuckle, not sure if he was over stepping his boundaries.

"You'll get your time to shine Bryce. Patience is the key."

"Well, at least I'm Bryce instead of Mr. Johnson, for a change."

He watched as P.O. Shawna Williams went about her normal task of jotting down his info. A few minutes later, she announced that they were done. She watched as Bundy rose out of his seat. "Next time you report, I'm going to be needing a urine sample, so you have more than enough time to study for your test."

Bundy nodded. Being that he was smoking like a chimney for the last few months, her humor wasn't as appreciated as she'd have liked it to be.

"Oh, and Mr. Johnson," Bundy spun around to face her. "When I take your urine this time, try not to flirt big fella." She even threw Bundy a wink, as he left her office wondering who was doing the flirting in the scene.

Now that Bundy had reached his plateau in the form of a Bentley and a decent stash, he felt it was time to give the one person in his life that matters the proper attention. Everything in the house was in order for Precious' arrival. This time, there were no expensive gifts. Everything that Bundy had done came from an act of pure unadulterated love. He had a picnic set up in the living room, and had the whole house surrounded by candles that gave off a romantic glow. Ironically, Precious walked through the front door as her Boo was in the process of lighting the last candle.

"Bryce, are you..." Precious stopped, and gasped. She was at a loss for words. Bryce walked up to her and embraced her while pressing his index finger against her lips.

"I'm realizing my priorities and getting them in order baby girl." He led Precious to the floor, and began giving her a back and foot massage, as the two conversed.

"I've been trying my best to maintain babe, but I'm starting to realize I'm hustling backwards." Precious couldn't help but think a negative connotation to the word 'hustle.' Even if it was in reference to something legal, she would have focused on that one word and had qualms about it. She was as square as they came. It was what Bryce loved about her. Precious brought about a balance in his life.

"I've been trying to get a little cash together so that we could start fresh, but every time I make a lil' progress, I start slipping." Precious cracked a smile. Bryce had no idea that she had him covered. All he had to do was come to his senses, and the rest of his plan would fall right into place.

Bryce began kneading into her thighs, sighing, "Right now, I just wanna enjoy your company. We can discuss our life together later.'"

After the massage, Bryce fed Precious from a basket full of fruit while tasting his choice of fruit from her body. He used a can of whipped cream to secure a slice of strawberry to her nipple, then sucked it up. A soft moan escaped Precious' lips. It felt like ages since Bryce had shown her body any type of affection.

He placed gentle love bites down her stomach, stopping at her navel, allowing his tongue to play in the center of her belly button. Precious' abdominal muscles went into spasms as she giggled. "That tickles." Before she could utter another word, Bryce was kissing his way down her thigh, and did the same to her other leg, before heading towards the 'promised land.'

Bryce placed a kiss directly on her clitoris, and held it between his lips as he used his tongue to beat a rise out of her love button. The next thing he knew Precious was grinding into his face as he held on to her hips for dear life.

"Umm hmm. Yes Bryce, yes!" Precious moaned, as she started to buck against Bryce's face uncontrollably. Bryce suppressed the smile he felt. It pleased him to know he was satisfying his woman in every way. He began to shake his head back and forth, never letting go of her clit, throwing in a few good slurps for effect. Precious' fingernails dug into the carpet, as she hissed, "Put it in me. I want you in me now!"

These were the words Bryce was waiting to hear as he moved on top of her, stopping midway to kiss her left nipple, before guiding his penis into her vagina.

"Oooh, yes," she purred. He began stroking her slowly, and deeply so she could feel every inch of his manhood. Before they knew it, they were sexing as if they hadn't touched each other since Bundy's release.

Precious took control, and started riding Bryce. She rode him in a reverse cowgirl position, so that he could have a bird's eye view of her ass as she ground into him. Bryce smacked her ass until it was cherry red. The aggression made Precious even wetter than she already was, as they bucked themselves through the carpet burns, and straight to orgasm.

"I'm cumming!" Bryce said it through gritted teeth as Precious pled, "No! Wait for me, I'm...I'm cumming toooo!" She squealed, as she collapsed alongside her lover. Before long, the two of them were laying in each other's arms, totally exhausted from their sweaty sex session.

"Precious, you sleep?" Precious looked up from where she was cradled in Bryce's arms.

"Not really. Why, what's up?"

"I've been doing a lot of thinking. I was wondering if you still want to relocate?"

Precious jumped up and smothered Bryce with kisses. The answer was self explanatory as far as he was concerned. For the longest, Precious was waiting for this moment. She was absolutely certain that a smaller town would calm Bryce down, and he had now given her the go ahead to test her theory. When she looked down, Bryce had a melancholic look about him.

"What's wrong?"

"Money. I wanted to leave wit' a lil' paper, but I think I'm better off cashing my chips in early,"

"Money? I wouldn't worry 'bout that. I got you covered," she smiled walking towards their bedroom to retrieve whatever it was that she had to show Bryce. When she came back, she sat down in front of him, crossed her legs, and laid out a small leather clad billfold with paperwork inside of it.

"What's that?" He nodded towards the billfold.

"Our future Bryce." Precious was cheesing from ear to ear. Her huge smile caused Bryce to do the same.

"Our future? Babe, what's going on?"

"If you give me a chance to, I'll tell you." Precious

turned to the first page. She proudly announced, "We are the proud owners of two twenty-four hour 'Wash-O- Mats' as well as a hair salon we co-own with my cousin Stacey. We own, well, it's sort of a bookstore, but it sells mixtapes and DVD's and magazines too."

"What do you mean, we? How?" Bryce was stumped. *Bundy was hyped.*

"What do you mean, how? All that money you were giving me. What did you think I was going to do with it, spend it?" Precious saw he was at a loss for words, so she explained. "You kept giving me the same amount Bryce. Fifteen thousand. By the third time, I started thinking that whatever you were doing, your luck was sure to run out. I invested in the Laundromat first, then another, and when I saw the money was still coming, I invested in Stacey's dream. The bookstore was her baby's father's idea. In total, we spent a little over sixty grand. The thing is, we've been making almost twenty thousand a month. Technically, you don't even have to work right now."

The smile on the big fella's face was enough for Precious to know she'd done good. *All Bundy could do was scoop her up.* Bryce made love to his baby girl one last time.

That night, Bundy's cell phone woke him out of his

sleep. When he answered, it was Michelle on the other end of the line. She sounded overly anxious about something. She was talking so fast, Bundy could barely make out her words. "Slow down 'Chelle, I can't hear shit you're saying."

"I need to speak to you right now!"

"Can't it wait 'till tomorrow?"

"No."

"Well can't you tell me now?"

"That's what I was trying to do, but..."

Bundy cut her short. "What is it Michelle?"

"Tina took me to this restaurant in Corona. As we were eating, this loud ass Spanish cat was in there stunting. One kid looked like the dude from the incident on Murdock, which made me pay them a little more attention than usual. To make a long story short, the kid referred to ole' boy as Fernando. I remember you mentioning..."

Bundy was no longer paying attention. Michelle had inadvertently found Fernando Morales.

Go or Get Even!

Chapter 13

The following morning...

*B*undy couldn't get a wink of sleep after Michelle's phone call. He tossed and turned all night, that one question nagging him; *should I just go and relocate or should I get even first?'*

He decided that he'd let fate answer the question by bringing the news to Yak, and agreeing with whatever he decided. Knowing Yak, Bundy would be dusting off his guns by nightfall. Bundy was already wondering if Fernando's new hideout could possibly be holding enough cash for him to make up for the proceeds that he lost at the Murdock Avenue spot.

Before he cracked the news to his homie Yak, Bundy needed to check Michelle's information for himself. He parked down the block from the Spanish restaurant located in the heart of Corona, Queens, and lit a blunt. When it came to getting money, or getting even, Bundy had the patience of a Buddhist monk. He would stay rooted to that spot across from the eatery until Fernando showed his face, or until daybreak, whichever came first. Being that Fernando knew exactly where to find him, Bundy had to assume Fernando knew what he looked like, so he laid low in the vehicle the whole time.

Three hours later, Bundy was pissing in a 7 Eleven 'big gulp' cup when out of nowhere, Fernando pulled up in a Mercedes SL with his entourage trailing behind him. Once they entered the restaurant, Bundy threw the cup to the curb, and started the engine to Precious' Toyota. He never told her that he didn't trade it in. He just had the car switched over to his name knowing that his Bentley was too flashy to creep in.

Twenty minutes later, Fernando and his team left the

restaurant and led Bundy to their new hideaway. Bundy checked for anything out of the ordinary for a few minutes before heading back to Jamaica, Queens to find Yak.

It seemed like Yak was avoiding Bundy. He wasn't answering any of his calls, and hadn't responded to any of the messages Bundy left on his voicemail. Bundy was too stubborn to give up his search. He sat in front of Yak's house in his newly acquired Bentley Convertible. Part of his reason for bringing the Bentley was to make Yak feel as if his absence was causing him to lose out on a shit load of paper.

"About fucking time!" Bundy barked, as he saw Yak making his way down the block with Joanna and Timmy. Bundy tapped the horn, causing Yak to squint in Bundy's direction until he finally realized who it was in the car.

"Aw hell nah! Is that you Bundy?"

"Yeah it's me nigga! Where you been at?"

"Shit, I know your ugly ass when I see you. I'm asking if the whip is you. You rolling 'round like you triple OG of cash money millionaires or sum' thin!" Yak ran his hand across the Tourneau cloth cover of the GT, and whistled.

"Damn! You been busy like a muh'fucka."

"Yeah, you know, I do what I can." Bundy was in full stunt mode. He was truly feeling himself. "Yak, where the fuck you been hiding at?"

"Chilling. Just trying to get my head right." Yak shrugged his shoulders.

That's when Bundy noticed Joanna and her son Timmy looking as if they were waiting on Yak. Bundy glanced at Yak's outfit. "Where you coming from all dressed up and shit?"

Yak had a smirk on his face knowing his answer was going to shock the big man. "I'm coming from church."

Bundy's eyebrow shot up and he gave Yak a quizzical look. He asked the one question he felt could explain Yak's sudden transformation. He nodded towards Joanna. "You fucking wit' shorty?"

Yak smiled. "Nah, it ain't like that. I'd never violate Clay like that." Bundy nodded, as Yak continued to explain. "Ever since the shootout, Joanna been hitting the church hard. I been going through some things ever since then, so I figured I'd keep her company and see what it's about."

"I can dig it, but today is Thursday."

"They had a gathering there, and we just coming back."

Yak knew Bundy wasn't much of a religious person. He figured his homie would view him attending church as a weakness. As if his close brush with death had turned him soft. The thought made it hard for Yak to look Bundy in the eye.

"We going to see Clay this weekend. He heard what happened, and I was surprised to hear his take on the situation. The man has really changed B. He's on some different shit. My nigga's getting his grown man on."

Bundy really wasn't trying to hear anything concerning Clay's metamorphosis. He wanted to know if Yak was ready to ride on Fernando.

"That's all good and well, but I've got some news for ya." Yak leaned into the Bentley. "I done found out where this nigga Fernando been hiding. You ready for some get back lil' homie?"

The look on Yak's face wasn't what Bundy was hoping for. Yak had a look that suggested he'd put the whole incident behind him, and was now counting his blessings.

"What? You just gonna let this nigga ride off into the sunset, knowing he done had his team put some hot ones in yo ' ass?"

Yak did a double take, hoping that Joanna could say something to save him from having to answer Bundy.

Timmy was the one who snapped him, momentarily, back to his priorities. "Hurry up Yak. My daddy 'posed to call us soon." Yak looked back and forth, unsure of what his next move should be. "Yo B, I gotta go."

"What time you want me to pick you up?" Bundy was, realizing, that the chance to get Fernando's money was slowly slipping from his grasp. Yak thought for a moment, and then looked back at Timmy, before answering, "Pick me up at midnight. I'll be in front of the crib." Yak sounded defeated. Everything he'd learned from the pastor at the church had just been tossed out the window.

"That's what the fuck I'm talking 'bout! That's the Yak I know." He peeled off before Yak could fuck up his plans and have a charge of heart.

Joanna could tell that there was definitely something bothering Yak.

Although he hadn't said a word since running into Bundy, Joanna was sure that their conversation had something to do with Yak's sudden mood change. Even Timmy felt the vibe, and at first, tried to snap Yak out of his funk by challenging him to a round of Madden '08 on his Playstation 3.

"C'mon Yak, I'm calling you out!" Yak glanced at the clock on the wall. It was 7P.M., half an hour before Clay was due to call. Yak played the game with Timmy until Clay's call came. After he spoke to Joanna and their son, Clay asked to speak to Yak.

"Clay, what's up witchu?"

"Everything's good youngster. How're you?" Clay joked. The two reminisced on old times, until Yak asked the question that was burning a hole in his conscience.

"Yo Clay, lemme ask you something."

"Shoot young blood." His choice of words made Yak flinch.

"When did you know that you were through wit' this gangsta shit?" For a minute there was silence, then Clay answered.

"I was almost going to tell you I just knew. But I realize now that it was a lot deeper than that. I think my epiphany came when I started to develop distaste for some of the same bullshit I used to advocate. After that, I think it's safe to say I just knew I didn't have it in me anymore." Clay knew Yak was going through that uncomfortable stage that came with turning one's life around.

"Listen Yak, it sounds to me like you're going through

some changes. I want you to keep one thing in mind lil'
homie. You only have one life to live, so live it to the
fullest. I'm in here wit' a shit load of cats, and the one
thing we all have in common is this; if we could do it all
over again, we would. And you best believe most of us
would leave out all the grimey shit."

"Yeah, but what about the enemies I'm leaving behind?
They ain't trying to hear all that goody two shoes shit.
Niggas got good memories, ya know? I got this one
situation that I been thinking 'bout fixing 'fore I do a one-
eighty. You feel me?"

"Oh yeah, I feel you. Don't go out like Carlito lil'
homie. If there is truly a Benny Blanco waiting 'round
the corner for yo' ass, then by all means, handle your
business. Just keep in mind, only you know which ones
are real beef, and which ones you can walk away from. I
gotta go Yak. Stay up my brother."

"No doubt. You do the same Clay."

After speaking to Clay, Yak retired to the basement
apartment of the two family house he shared with Joanna.
He needed to do some serious soul searching.

A half hour into his thoughts, Joanna tapped on the
door. "Yak, I was wondering if you were hungry." Joanna
walked in on Yak cleaning his guns. A can of WD-40 lay

on the bed beside him. He said nothing. Joanna sat his food on the dresser and left him alone.

By the time midnight came, Bundy and O were already in front of Yak's crib in Precious' old Toyota. When Yak came outside, Bundy could see that his heart wasn't in it. Bundy's mind couldn't get past the hope of securing a chunk of Fernando's cash. As soon as the three of them pulled off, Candy pulled up to the front of Joanna's house. She knocked on the basement door so hard, the sound caused Joanna to appear at her upstairs window.

"Candy? Is that you?"

"Yeah, I'm looking for Yak."

Joanna nodded for Candy to come around front so that she could let her in. Once Candy entered the house, Joanna could sense that she was stressed out. Usually, Candy was meticulous when it came to her appearance. At the moment, she looked disheveled. She was pacing in Joanna's living room as if she didn't know where to start. Joanna helped her out.

"Candy, Yak just left with Bundy and O"

"I have to speak to him."

"Why, what happened?"

"I don't know, I just got this feeling something bad is 'bout to happen, and my vibe tells me it's gonna happen to my baby."

Joanna could see that whatever premonition Candy might have thought she had, there was no convincing her that it wasn't real. Joanna handed her the phone but Candy shook her head. "I already tried. It just keeps going to voicemail."

The entire time they sat across from Fernando's hideaway, Bundy kept glancing at Yak. He was looking for any signs that Yak was having second thoughts, or the jitters. Yak sat there like a piece of emotionless steel. O noticed that not only did he stay silent; he hardly blinked the whole time they were waiting. When O went to turn on the radio, Yak's hand shot out and turned it off. O looked at Bundy, who shook his head as if telling him to let it be.

"Showtime!" Bundy said, as he spotted Fernando and his entourage pull up to their new spot. What Bundy hated most about their present locale, was the entrance to it. It was one of those double doors that led to a basement of a building; the kind that bodegas had to open when their deliveries came.

They watched Fernando and the rest of his team march their way inside and close the doors behind them. That's when O asked the magic question. "So how ya'll wanna do this?" Yak was checking his Rugers one last time, while Bundy and O debated whose plan was best.

"I say we toss a brick through the nigga's Benz window, and when the alarm starts ringing and them dudes come out, we start blasting."

O shook his head. "Let's just knock on the door and see what happens." Bundy looked at him like he was stupid.

At that moment, a prostitute walked up with a Spanish john on her arm, tapped on the door, and the two went inside. Yak said nothing, as he got out of the car and walked around the corner to Northern Boulevard. Bundy knew the look on Yak's face and uttered to O, "C'mon, we're following his lead."

They stayed back as they observed Yak solicit the services of one of the streetwalkers who would lead them to Fernando's underground whorehouse. Bundy and O hid in the bushes.

When Yak reached the bottom of the stairs, he noticed two men by the bar. One dove for cover, as the second

tried to reach for his gun. Yak hit him with a single shot to
the head. Meanwhile, O pulled out two Uzi's and tapped
them together. "Nigga, you watch too many movies,"
Bundy mumbled.

The two of them jumped down the whole flight of
stairs, just in time to get the man who dove from behind
the bar, now trying to get a bead on Yak. O let off half
a dozen shots in the man's torso, killing him on sight.
"Who's watching too many movies now, muh'fucker?"

Bundy noticed how reckless Yak was moving. He
headed towards the back of the whorehouse like he was
the only person in the spot with a gun. It almost seemed as
if Yak didn't even care about dying.

"What's up wit' Yak? He thinks he bulletproof or sum'
thin?"

They followed Yak to the back of the spot, barely able
to keep up. Yak kicked in the first door and saw a man
pulling up his pants while one of the hoes lay cowering
under the bed. Yak was trying to figure out if the man
was a customer or one of Fernando's hired thugs. When it
seemed to take too much figuring out, Yak shot him in the
face and moved to the next room. Bundy and O were busy
laying down gunfire towards the men at the end of the hall
who were trying their best to get at Yak.

"Fernando! Es Moreno..." The man was chopped down before he could finish the sentence. Bundy kept firing, trying his best to catch up to Yak. By then, Yak was at the end of the hall. Fernando peeked out just enough to catch a glimpse of Bundy. The fact that none of them had on masks told Fernando the one thing he feared. They were there to kill him and did not plan on leaving any witnesses. Whatever chica that didn't have enough sense to hightail it out of there at the first burst of gunfire, was chopped down by O's Uzi.

When Yak kicked in the final door at the end of the hall, the sight before him caused him to hesitate. Fernando's ex-girlfriend and servant Melina was in the corner cowering like she had an extreme case of the shakes. What really caught Yak's attention was the extreme abuse she'd obviously been subjected to. There were bruises covering her arms and legs. Slashes and whelps all over her back. From the wall, a chain hung which led to a metal collar around Melina's neck. Heavy enough to cause the cracked chaffing he noticed around her neck area. Underneath her was a puddle mixed with blood, urine, and what smelled like feces. The room was too rank for Yak to distinguish one odor from another. The sight caused a tear to fall from Yak's eye, and he remembered the Pastor's sermon from the last time he'd met with Joanna's congregation at the church.

"Most of us, when we think of the sins we have committed, do not consider the fact that our sins have a domino effect. For every action, there is a reaction. See, the drug dealer may acknowledge the harm he is doing to his customer, the addict. But he does not know of the child at home hungry, because Mamma spent the last of their food money on getting high. The stick-up boys don't know that when they caught that father or husband coming out of the check cashing place for his paycheck. They just got a family that much closer to getting evicted. They just think how good those new Jordan's are going to look on their feet. I implore the younger generation to consider..."

"Yak, look out!" By the time Yak realized what was going on, it was too late. Fernando had stuck his arm around the corner, and squeezed a shot that found its way directly into Yak's temple. For some reason, Yak knew on impact, that there would be no surviving this time around. On his way to the floor, Yak smiled, as he realized what they meant by your life flashing before you when you die.

He wished that he could tell Bundy that what actually flashed before you was your conscience. It was more like a two second mini version of Judgment Day. He glanced at Melina one last time on his way down. Getting a flash-back of the act he'd forced her to do to Fernando, which she was suffering for ever since.

'C'mon Yak, I'm calling you out!' Timmy had the controller in his hand, but this time there was a white light around him, and angel wings. He could hear Timmy as plain as day. Then he heard the Pastor. *'God is trying to tell you something,'* he shouted. *He was trying to tell me that Timmy was 'posed to save me, but I ain't pay attention to the signs.* A tear escaped Yak's eye, as he heard Timmy's voice for a second time. *'Hurry up Yak. My Daddy 'posed to call us soon!'* This time, the voice didn't sound like Timmy's. He saw a bright light before everything went black.

"Yaakkkk!" Bundy let off half a clip as Fernando tried to run, but got clipped in the leg. When all the dust had settled, Bundy was standing over Fernando with his trademark Desert Eagle pointed dead at the kingpin's head.

"Any last words Fernando?"

"Listen, if you let me live..."

"Not happening." Bundy squeezed the fatal shot that left Fernando a corpse.

"Aw shit!" Bundy heard O shout. When he walked

over, he saw one of Fernando's gunmen with a stomach wound. The man was coughing up blood, and his future didn't look so bright. What really caused O to curse was the police badge the man was clutching in his left hand.

"This nigga's a cop." A few feet away, a second dirty cop was crawling over to his partner's aid. The partner had a blood stain in his crotch area.

Bundy uttered indifferently, "And?" followed by a shot to the head of the cop. Bundy looked at O who knew the rules to the game all too well.

O shrugged. "Fuck 'em! Co-defendants to the end," as he riddled the partner in the face with bullets. The two of them didn't even bother to search for currency. Once Fernando had killed Yak, the gunfight was no longer business. It was personal.

By the next morning, Bundy was a mess. O had done the smart thing and skipped town. Bundy, on the other hand, was in his living room nursing a bottle of Hennessy. He was grateful that Precious had gone to work early, because he was in no mood to face her. He didn't have the heart to face anyone for that matter. He avoided his phone which was ringing off the hook between Candy's and Joanna's numbers. He didn't know what to do with himself. That was when he heard the doorbell ring.

Bundy grabbed hold of his Desert Eagle, and briefly noted that it was the same gun that now had bodies on it. "Fuck it," he growled, snatching the door open. He stared at the person in front of him for a few seconds before realizing it was Chico.

Chico looked inside the house, then glanced around the block before stating his business. "Listen, I'm not here to lecture you or nothing, just to give you this." Chico thrust an envelope full of cash in Bundy's hand, adding, "you're hot as fish grease right now partner. Your best bet is to kick rocks and bounce to a nice, small, quiet town 'til the heat blows over." Chico leaned in to whisper, "Dirty cops always tell they mans when things are going down, so that they could cover their ass just in case. You just became the just in case, so be on point. They might be gunning fa' you, and these cats ain't nothing but thugs wit' badges to hide behind." Chico was gone, just as quick as he came.

When Bundy told Precious he wanted to leave town immediately, her response was just as immediate. Just knowing that Yak had lost his life was enough for Precious to know that now wasn't the time for questions. When they got where they were going, then maybe she'd play the twenty questions game. As of now, the two of them were packing their necessities and would send for the rest later.

The hardest part of their departure was when Bundy had to convince Precious to leave without him. "Why, we can just leave together. Whatever you did, it would look a lot better if you were traveling with a companion as opposed to being alone."

"Precious, I don't have time to argue with you. Now go!" He pecked her on the cheek, and made his way out the house. Bundy needed to tie up any loose ends he may have left behind. He got on his cell phone and asked Chico if he could get his P.O. off his back for a while. Since his crimes weren't public, Chico felt it was within his power to give it a try.

Afterwards, Bundy called Michelle. Since the two of them had put in work together, he wanted to make sure that Michelle was properly prepped in case the Detectives came to question her concerning him.

"Chelle, I'm right near your crib. I need to holler at you."

"I don't stay at Tina's no more. That bitch been acting too shady fa' me lately. I'm a block down at my cousin Toya's. You remember the house right?"

"Yeah, I'll see you in a few." As Bundy was going past, he saw Sosa with a duffle bag slung over his shoulder. It wasn't the bag that made Bundy question 'Sosa's appearance, but the way he was moving. Sosa was moving as if he was up to no good. Bundy knew the look from experience, and couldn't help but park Precious' Toyota to see what his former crimee was up to.

Bundy thought *how he'd purchased the red Bentley, but had to ride in the Toyota most of the time, due to the fact that the flashy red convertible didn't coincide with his occupation as a stick-up kid.* He spotted Tina come to the door and let Sosa in. Scanning the block just as leery as Sosa had done, before slamming her door shut. Bundy's mind was convinced that something was up.

What you two up to? Bundy grinned, sneaking around the back of Tina's crib, and on top of the garbage can that would expose him to Tina's bedroom window. Although the window's blinds were closed, Bundy was able to see through an exposed corner of the blind. His eyes damn near popped out of his head when he saw Sosa counting stacks of cash from the duffle bag. He put his ear to the slightly cracked window, trying to hear whatever it was he'd obviously missed in the time he'd been home.

"I still can't believe you pulled this shit off Sosa." Tina was so amped off the sight of so much paper, Bundy had no problem hearing her.

"Tina, *we* pulled this off. I'm giving you your props. I didn't think the shit was gonna fall our way for a minute. I originally planned to be around when Bundy touched down, but by the time I seen him, him and Yak were inseparable. Them catching Fernando for three bricks didn't help my cause either. I got the boot due to their come up." Sosa was able to laugh at it now because he was the one holding all the cards at the moment. He was busy counting the money from the Murdock Avenue spot, as well as Fernando's cash. It made Sosa think of another unplanned perk from his plan.

"I had to cop from Fernando's punk ass, and now that he's gone, I ain't gotta pay that back either. Life is so fucking sweet sometimes. My dumb ass thought Bundy had Chico in the smash, and my paranoia done hit me the jackpot."

"Letting Bundy think Fernando and 'em came at them

a second time was brilliant too Sosa." Tina was stroking 'Sosa ego trying to ensure that she got broken off a little something for her troubles.

"Nah, I'll tell you what's brilliant the way you took Michelle to the restaurant so that she'd see lil' Pito wit' Fernando and 'em. I knew she was gonna tell that oversized circus clown. But I ain't gonna lie, I ain't think he'd be able to body that nigga."

"And two cops? That shit is crazy!"

Sosa shrugged. "Crazy? That shit is lovely. That fool is long gone by now. Good riddance too. I'm finna take over Corona, and get Murdock back popping!"

"That was some real Keizer Soze shit Sosa, fa real. How'd you know it would work?" Tina asked. She was thinking she was getting a front row view on how the game was played.

"I didn't. Matter of fact, it wasn't really planned. I just sat at the Player's Lounge and I guess that was the best thing them fools did, 'cause now that I was forced off the block, I plugged into Fernando. I saw he was arrogant, and I played to his ego like you're doing to mines now." Sosa continued counting the money, which didn't slow him down from running his jibs.

"It didn't take long for me to get in tight. You'd be

surprised how much you hear just standing on the sidelines." Sosa let out a high pitched chuckle, as he counted off another stack. "That nigga Bundy was the worst though. Anytime he caught a good jux, he would upgrade his whip. So your updates, and hearing at the club that big baller got caught slipping, pretty much helped me put two and two together." Sosa started to throw money in the air, making it rain. He was too caught up with patting himself on the back to notice the door to Tina's bedroom flying off the hinges.

"What the..." Before Sosa could manage to get his sentence out, the sight of Bundy and his .50 Caliber Desert Eagle got the words caught in his throat. Sosa didn't even try and cop a plea, he just shook his head.

"You're too smart for your own good Sosa. Tell Fernando I send my regards." The single shot to 'Sosa heart was followed by an ear deafening boom. Tina started to scream, but the second shot prevented her from doing so. "You can share the maggots with him, you bum bitch!"

Bundy scooped up the cash, and was out. He didn't even bother to stop by Michelle's. He was on the nearest highway, making a beeline for Precious and their new home.

Chapter 14

Starting Anew!

A couple of months later...

$\mathcal{B}$undy and Precious had decided to settle down in the prestigious suburbs of Atlanta, Buckhead to be exact. Bundy had it confused with T.I.'s hometown of Bankhead, and had asked the realtor if she was showing them a house in the 'hood.

"Oh no, Mr. Johnson Your wife was very specific as to what you were looking for."

When Bundy had seen the oversized Colonial spread with pillars at the threshold, he knew he and Precious had found their dream home. Bundy felt as if that day was only yesterday, as he made his way down the cul-de-sac of his neighborhood and onto the main street.

Although Bundy was trying his best to behave himself, he still found himself rolling his Bentley GTC through the poorest ghettoes Atlanta had to offer. He wanted to see what their 'hood was about. The corner boys were pointing at Bundy's vehicle every time he came through, hoping to one day come up like the man in the coupe. At the same time, Bundy was hoping their bosses would show their face in the event he needed a come up of his own.

Damn, you niggas looking like food to me! Bundy thought all of the ATL hustlers were mentally slower than his New York brethren. The one thing he had to respect was the fact that damn near every last one of them were packing some form of hardware. He shook off the old thoughts that ran through his head, reminding himself that he and Precious were there to start anew.

He parked the GTC in front of the corner store and got out to purchase a cigar for the bag of weed he had in his pocket.

A kid wearing a New Era fitted cap to the side asked, "Damn pimping, that you?" Bundy ignored the youth, causing his homies to break out in laughter. "Odell, you got to sell an awful lot of weed to lean in one o' dem thangs patna!"

Bundy copped the cigars, and on his way out, noticed that the same car he peeped a block ago, was still tailing him. For a moment, he thought one of the ATL boys had finally gotten up enough heart to try him. Part of him was itching for some drama anyway, since he felt the town was too slow for his taste. Aside from the few New Yorkers that had relocated, he felt like an outsider in a foreign land. He pulled up a few blocks away and waited for his followers to make their move.

By the time they turned the corner, they saw Bundy leaning against his whip with his arms folded. Since the jig was up, the two men decided to use the direct approach. "Mr. Johnson? Or should we just call you Bundy?" One of the men flashed a New York City Detective badge.

"Aren't you guys out of your jurisdiction?"

"Oh, I guess you'd be right if we were here on official business," the first cop chided. "Actually, our business out here is more of a personal nature."

Bundy glanced around the area, calculating his chances

of getting away with breaking up two cops. He knew the area somewhat, but wasn't sure if he could get away with it clean. The last thing he wanted to do was bring attention to himself.

"You ain't got no bidness wit' me."

Bundy turned returning to his car when one of the officers, blurted out, "I guess you're sort of right, but we're here for an old comrade, Fernando." The look on Bundy's face answered the next question. "You remember him, right? He used to employ a few friends of mine."

"Off the books of course." The second cop jumped in. "Risky stuff, no benefits, no 401K. So we gotta make our own retirement funds."

"That's where you come in Mr. Johnson. Since you wanna start anew, and ride off into the sunset with Ms. Precious Davis, we're gonna need a chunk of hush money for all those widows you left back in New York."

Bundy was about to curse the officers out, when one of them uttered, "Take a few days to think about it. When I call have a quarter mil in cash ready, or it's gonna cost you a lot more patna." Bundy went to reach for his .357, but the cop warned, "I wouldn't do that. Our third man is babysitting your Precious, and if we don't get back safely he's bound to run up in Peachtree Mall and cause a bloodbath in that lil' business you guys own."

Bundy knew they weren't bluffing if they knew of the clothing store they owned in the mall.

"Like I said we'll be in touch."

"Loser!" His Partner ended the sentence for him.

Meanwhile, back in New York; the Police were pressing Chico, Deuce, and any other name that came up as a possible lead in the murder of the two Detectives found dead in a Corona brothel. The influx of information provided by snitches was mostly based on rumors and innuendoes. Some were so far off the mark that the officers didn't even bother to check up on them. Some were pretty close. Usually, a crooked cop knew enough inside details to distinguish which leads were credible. They'd only been at it a few weeks, and had heard it all. The Detectives at the 110th Precinct were sitting around discussing the various tales they'd heard, while some played nonchalant trying to ear hustle a decent version to go off.

"Check this out. I got a C.I. in Corona who was telling me that this whole mess is based on a club out in Harlem that was selling weight to all the hustlers in the tri-state, then turning around and robbing them back for the drugs."

"I can top that one. My C.I. claims that some notorious ex-kingpin came home and decided that whatever crew didn't set him out, he was simply going to take his."

"Mine is similar. The kingpin in question owned the club, but was at war with some Colombians who didn't appreciate their throats being cut by some 'Morenos,' so they killed one of the kingpin's soldiers, thus, starting an all out war."

All of the Detectives started laughing. Detective Jones had enough. He banged his fist on the table, causing the whole precinct to turn quiet. "What the fuck is so funny? We got two Detectives dead. Dirty cop rumors or not, I would hope if it was me in the meat wagon, you idiots would try a lil' harder than sitting around giggling like schoolgirls."

"Well what you expect us to do?"

"I'm glad somebody had the decency to ask." Jones pulled out his scratch pad. "Between the lines of every rumor lies a small detail of truth gentlemen. All of your C.I.'s versions have one or two things in common, the first being the club. We know there is a club, so we start there and see if we can get to the second common factor, which is," he flipped to another page in his scratch pad. "This ex-kingpin, whoever he is, is definitely the one person causing all this havoc."

Kingpin or not, he is the one behind all of the dead bodies. The kid found at the whorehouse was shot prior to this, in a similar fashion. He was definitely in the middle of some type of drug or turf war. Instead of comparing punch lines you morons should be running the name."

Jones flipped through his pad a third time until he found what he was looking for, Yak's government name, Todd Branch. "See what known acquaintances you come up with. The kid's got a record, so check it, and cross reference his co-defendants to our computer database. While you're at it, have a visit to this club. I'm sure somebody has a name for this establishment."

"The rumor is your establishment supplies half of the drugs for the tri-state area. Now, if this is indeed a bunch of bullshit, I'm sure a businessman such as yourself doesn't want his source of income under the scrutiny of law enforcement. So why not help us out?" The Detectives from the 110th Precinct were trying to press Chico for any type of lead that could help them in their investigation.

All Chico was thinking about was what type of business he could invest in now that the Player's Lounge was hot.

"If I could be of help Officer, I would. I pay taxes like every other citizen." Chico emphasized the word citizen.

"You know, we could really bust your balls over the way this club is set up. You don't have a liquor license for the private part of the spot, nor a gambling license. I'm sure most of your dealings here aren't in accordance with the City's guidelines."

"I understand sir. To be honest, a fine is relatively small in comparison to the charges you are insinuating. I'd much rather take my chances with the Player's Lounge getting shut down." Chico got out of his seat, and escorted the officers to the door. "If that is all gentlemen, I have a busy day ahead of me."

As, they left, the officer asking all the questions mumbled, "We'll be in touch slick. This thing ain't over by a long shot. We're gonna be all over you guys asses until we get who we're lookin' for."

"Baby, let's go to the club. I feel like partying tonight."

"Huh? Oh, aight. Whatever!" Bundy was barely paying

attention to Precious, his mind was on the two Officers he'd encountered earlier in the day.

"Did you hear a word I just said?" Precious pressed him.

"Yeah, you said you wanna hit a club, right?"

Precious huffed, as she repeated the part Bryce had missed. "I said, get dressed. We have to meet Tammy there at ten." Tammy was the only person Precious knew in ATL. She had relocated about a year ago.

Chapter 15

Epilogue

"Bryce, telephone!" Bundy cursed. He was trying to get ready for his night on the town, and didn't feel like running his jibs on the phone. The only reason he didn't ignore the call was because the only people who had the number were a few trusted individuals. He wanted the smoke to clear from the chaos he left back in New York before he let every Tom, Dick, and Harry know his whereabouts.

One of those trusted few was Chico. He was the one

who talked Bundy's P.O., Shawna Williams, into doctoring his paperwork to look as if she'd given him permission to relocate.

"Hello?" Bundy answered the phone.

"Big Fella! What's happening?" It was O.

"Ain't shit, and you?"

"I just got a rare package from my uncle L. I should've known his cheap ass wasn't sending me all them white tees, 'cause the note said to give your big ass half." O was telling Bundy in code, that the drugs he'd gotten from Sosa were sold, and to be on the lookout for his cut of the cash. Bundy was already sitting on the three hundred grand he'd gotten from Sosa after killing him and Tina.

"Yo, did you hear 'bout Chico and Deuce?"

"Nah, what happened?"

"Them niggas done started a record label, son."

The news made Bundy smile. After all the years he'd held a grudge against Chico, Bundy now discovered him to be his biggest ally.

"Word? Yo, tell 'em I said to rep Murdock like the second coming of LL."

"O laughed, adding, "If Deuce was Cut Creator, and Chico was L, I guess you'd be like Bimmy. Dudes would be like, 'they label fucking wit' them gangstas!"

"I ain't fucking wit' that one O" Bundy couldn't help but laugh. "So what you up to?" he asked O.

"I don't wanna jinx it right now, but you'll be the first to know if it goes through."

"You gonna do me like that, son?"

"I'll tell you this much. If I pull it off, we'll be known as the 'Corporate Kingpins' from here on out."

"Bryce, you ready?" Precious called out.

"Yo O, I'm gonna holler atchu later."

"Aight son. One!"

"One!"

The one thing Bundy noticed about Atlanta's club scene was the fact that it wasn't much different from New York. He had to admit that the women were a lot healthier. The average girl was what would be considered 'thick' in New York. They were also more bold and aggressive in their approach. Between his Bentley, Rolex, and New York City swagger, Bundy was the talk of the club. Women were slipping him their number on the sly, and Bundy, being his usual self, took them.

As he waited at the bar for his drink, a local baller by the name of King walked up on Bundy and started conversing out of the blue. "Homie, you got New York City written all over you." Bundy turned, half interested, until he saw the stacks of cash King was placing on the bar.

"Name's King." He bumped fists with Bundy, who scanned the area immediately noticing two bodyguards not far from King. King peeped Bundy's move, and it made him all the more sure of the proposition he had in mind for the towering New Yorker. King whispered in the barmaid's ear and a minute later the DJ was announcing that King was buying out the bar. He now had Bundy's full attention.

"So, how you like ATL so far?"

"It's all right." Bundy glanced at the watch on King's wrist, and was already doing a mental appraisal.

"Not to be nosy, but you got any plans out here?" King was straight to the point, as usual.

"Well, I ain't looking to set up shop, nor step on any toes, if that's what you mean?"

King shook his head. "Nah." King realized he didn't get a name from Bundy. "I didn't catch your name."

"I didn't throw it, but the name is Bundy." Bundy tipped his drink towards King. "Since, you're buying and all."

King nodded and smiled, as he handed Bundy a hundred dollar bill with his cell phone number written on it. "No bullshit Bundy. I'm looking for a good dude who can represent my team by networking some out of town moves. I know niggas respect strength patna, and you look like you can hold your own. If you in, gimme a call." King gave the waitress a signal, and before Bundy knew it, he was being passed two bottles of 'Ace of Spades.'

No matter where you go, there you are, Bundy thought, grinning as he rubbed his palms together. He was already contemplating three things, how long it would take for him to get King to trust him, just how much money King was worth, if he should contact O, or try this one last jux on his own? *Stickin' & movin' baby. It ain't over 'till it's over!* He could feel the adrenaline pumping through his veins, as his trigger finger began to itch.

When he returned to his table, Precious peeped the two bottles of 'Ace of Spades.' "Who was that guy you were talking to at the bar Bryce?"

Bundy slid back into his seat, drank straight from the bottle, and wiped his mouth with his sleeve. "Hopefully, my new best friend baby girl."

Coming Soon...

So Hard 2 Change

V.I.P. International's Main Office...

"Tarsha, can you come into my office for a minute?" The intercom clicked off before she could respond.

"Awww damn," Tarsha mumbled. She was just settling into her new position at V.I.P. International. She liked the lifestyle her receptionist salary afforded her. Before, the only support Tarsha was getting for herself and her eight year old son, Tyriek was a monthly check from the city.

I knew I should have called, she thought chastising herself as she made her way to the boss' office. Tarsha was trying to figure out a way to explain her tardiness. It was her second time this week. Although her boss seemed down to earth, she didn't want to get in the habit of taking Mr. Johnson's kindness for weakness.

I'm just gonna be straight up and explain that my son is sick, and that the sitter stood me up. She took a deep breath before entering the office. When she stepped inside, there was an assortment of liquor bottles scattered across the conference table. Tarsha could tell that they were empty. Before she could inquire about this odd scenario, Bryce Johnson supplied the answer to satisfy her curiosity.

"Tarsha, I've been waiting on you."

"Mr. Johnson, I can explain."

Bryce cut her off. "It's not that serious. Can I get your opinion on something?" He pointed to the array of liquor bottles. For the first time since entering the office, Tarsha noticed that the bottles all bore the company name. "O is starting a premium line of the Me'nage brand. Since Hennessy has the VSOP, he wants to make a Me'nage V.O. What I want to know from you is which of these bottles look like they can justify a hundred and sixty-five dollar price tag?"

Tarsha looked at the first bottle and shook her head from side to side. "Nah?"

Bryce asked her to elaborate.

"It looks too much like Cristal. If a person wanted Cristal, then they'd just order it. You want to keep your originality." Bryce nodded in agreement.

"This one is so loud it looks tacky." She giggled at the fuchsia colored bottle with the pink bow on it.

"Yeah. That one was O's choice. He would pick some flamboyant shit, ya know?"

"What does the V.O. stand for?"

"Vintage Original."

"Sounds good to me." Tarsha stepped in front of a black tinted bottle with gold Old English lettering, and gold foil encasing the top. "I like this one. It has class and flavor."

"Perfect. That was my choice too." They both nodded and the silence that followed led Tarsha to believe her services were no longer needed for the moment. She pondered on bringing up her lateness, but pushed past the urge and excused herself. As soon as her hand hit the doorknob, Bryce called out to her.

"Oh, and Tarsha." She turned around with a guilt ridden look on her face. "I know how hard it is raising a son." Then Bryce caught himself. "Well, I'm about to know. In the future, if you need more time to get things at home in order; don't be afraid to talk to me about it."

Tarsha felt as if he'd read her mind. What she didn't know was that O had a video camera installed right outside their office. Lucky for Bryce, Tarsha also had the habit of speaking her thoughts aloud.

Outside of his office, Bryce saw Tarsha leaning against the door with a relieved look on her face. 'Mr. Johnson, you are a real dude," she muttered to herself.

Bryce turned off the audio and video. He only kept it on during the hour before Tarsha arrived for work. After that, he knew she would alert him of anyone that entered his place of business, whether they had an appointment or not.

Bryce thought about Tarsha's statement. He figured what was the point of him hiring a sister, if he was going to ride her like he was 'the other man.' Bryce chuckled, realizing that he was speaking from his own prejudices. When Tarsha referred to Bryce as a real dude, she had no idea how accurate she was.

It hadn't even been a full two years since Bryce had been released from Auburn Correctional Facility after almost doing a five year bid.

You've come a long way nigga, Bryce thought. It seemed like just yesterday he was reliving the tyranny he'd brought home from bearing a chip on his shoulder which brought his penchant for violence to the forefront. *'Stickin & Movin'*, robbing every hustler that he deemed worthy of his blood, sweat, and barrel of his .50 Desert Eagle. It was this very penchant that caused him to lose his childhood friend, and comrade-in-arms, Yak.

Just as he was beginning to lose himself in the moment, the intercom snapped him out of his reverie.

"Mr. Johnson, Chico's on line two."

"Put him through Tarsha."

"Mr. Johnson, huh? I ain't gonna lie Bundy," Chico chuckled, "it's been a while now, and it still takes some getting used to. Bundy in the corporate world! Niggas on Murdock still think I'm making that shit up.

"Well, this leopard done changed his spots Chico."

"More like a wolf. They can house train a wolf, but if

they play too rough muh'fuckers will discover that the wolf still has its fangs and claws."

"True, true," Bundy laughed, changing the subject.

"So, what's good Chico? I know you ain't calling this early unless you've got some important shit to drop on a nigga."

"We 'bout to shoot Big East's video on Murdock. LL is gonna come through since he was the original Queens cat to do a video on 'the rock."

Big East was the premiere artist on Chico and Deuce's label 'Corporate Kingpins.' The term 'Corporate Kingpins' was derived from the two men's refusal to give up on their dreams of making the transition from the block to the boardrooms of Corporate America. Their first merger, The Player's Lounge, was shut down due to law enforcement officials applying pressure once they suspected them of funneling drugs through the club. The pressure caused Chico and Deuce to fold and switch their venture to the music industry.

"We're gathering every last one of Queens' finest for the video." Chico rambled off a list of the borough's bell ringers. "Dolla Bill, Rob, Lo, Prince and Graf. Everybody's coming through!"

"Okay, so watchu want me to do?"

"I want you and O to make an appearance. Bring some cases of Me'nage. So we can do this shit up Q-borough style!"

"A'ight, we'll be there." Bryce was reluctant, but saw an opportunity to do some cross marketing in the form of free advertisement.

"That's what's up! My people will come through later with the V.I.P passes. One!"

"A'ight. One!"

It only took a few seconds before he was back to reflecting on his past. He wondered what his femme fatale and partner-in-crime, Michelle had been up to. As well as the old mob from Murdock Avenue. Ever since his wife, Precious had gotten pregnant, Bryce no longer played the streets. He had an addiction to the 'hood. He feared any contact with Queens' major players, would easily cause the beast in him to resurface.

When the front door to his office flew open, Bryce knew that it could not have been any other than his business partner O.

"Wake up nigga! We've got a big day ahead of us." He threw an envelope containing their invites on the table, announcing, "Today's the day, big dawg."

O was referring to the award ceremony for Black Enterprises 'Entrepreneur of the Year Award'. Bryce, O, and Me'nage liquor had been named recipients of this year's award, and were scheduled to receive the award, later on in the evening.

"I've got my speech memorized, we good to go kicko!"

"Damn! I almost forgot about that shit. I wasn't really in the mood to fuck with it anyway," Bryce griped.

"C'mon Scrappy. Don't do this to me." O was being his usual melodramatic self. "You've become a real home body ever since the wife's pregnancy."

His words brought a smile to Bryce's lips. "O, I'm not saying I won't go. I'm just admitting that I'd much rather have a night at home with the misses."

"You mean another night at home wit' the misses." O shot back. The retort caused Bryce to change the subject.

"Yo, I just spoke to Chico on the phone." Before he could finish, O was nodding his head, letting Bryce know that he'd already received the news of Big East's video shoot.

"I'm already on it. We gon' put the new line of premium V.O. in the video."

"How *we* gon' do that if the juice ain't ready?"

"Fuck the juice! We got the bottles. We'll just put water in the bottles.

It ain't like anyone watching the video is gonna know."

"You got a point. Anyway, I'm gonna cut the day short, and go pick up my tux. After lunch, don't expect to see me around."

Bryce did as promised, and was headed towards the underground parking to retrieve his burgundy Maserati, by noon.

When he stuck his key in the door, he was surprised to find two men from his past staring him dead in the face. They were the two corrupt cops that worked for the now deceased Fernando Morales, a Corona, Queens's drug lord who had gone to war with Bundy and his group of stick-up kids.

No matter how hard Bryce tried to go legit, the officers on Fernando's old payroll could only see Bryce as the notorious Bundy who was responsible for their boss' death. They intended to make him pay for the extravagant lifestyle Fernando was no longer able to provide due to his demise. They had already tried to extort money from Bryce/Bundy back when he had relocated to Atlanta. Bundy thought they'd given up on trying to muscle their way into his pockets; that is, until today.

"Long time no see, Mr. Johnson. Or should I call you Bundy?"

"What do you want?" Bryce was in no mood for games.

"Our money. Ain't shit change, boy!"

"I got your boy right here!" Bundy grabbed a handful of his testicles, accentuating his point.

One of the officers walked towards the car, as Bundy clenched his fists ready to brawl. The officer leaned in to his shoulder and placed a card on the hood of his whip. "I'll be expecting a call from you before midnight. You're back in our town now, so don't be stupid enough to ignore us, like you did in ATL."

Bundy grilled them both, as he ripped the card up in their face. They threw a second card at him, snarling. "The price we asked for in Atlanta, just doubled, asshole!"

"I remember back in the days, LL Cool J had everyone in Queens wearing Troop sneakers, with the matching velour sweats. So, me and Bryce were out on Merrick Boulevard near 'Pop & Kim's. The store RUN-DMC made famous by shouting them out as the official ice cold forty ounce spot. It was September, and was way too cold for the sweat suits. Our boy XL suggested we get a bottle of Cisqo to warm us up. Well the drink tasted like a spiked glass of kool-aid, leading us to believe that a few bottles would do nothing to us." The crowd started snickering, because most of them were fully aware of the kick-ass effects of the wine cooler.

"See! Ya'll remember that, huh? That lit' bottle put my big buddy out. We dropped him off at the steps of his crib, and his mom found him foaming at the mouth. Well, she didn't actually find him we had rung the doorbell and ran." The crowd started roaring with laughter at O's moment of nostalgia.

"Never would I have thought that years later we'd have our own line of liquor." He hefted the award above his head. "Thank you Black Enterprise for recognizing the lil' man!"

After the ceremony was over, O suggested that he and Bryce go out to celebrate.

"Nah, I'm gonna call it a night." He glanced at his wife, Precious. "Go 'head Bryce. I'll be alright."

O's face lit up. "Yeah bro', let's do it up tonight."

"Nah, I'm good."

"Aight, I'm out then." They all went their separate ways.

"You could have gone," Precious told Bryce once they were inside the car.

"I know, but I'd rather chill with you. Besides, I'm gonna rub you down wit' cocoa butter. See if we can reduce the chances of you getting stretch marks, cause if you not looking sexy, I might be tempted to find me a lil' young girl to take up the slack." Bryce joked.

"Very funny, I'm sure a few stretch marks won't stop me from finding a sugar daddy out there," Precious shot back.

"Aight, no more jokes." As they pulled off, Bryce glanced at his wife, who was rubbing her belly.

"Bryce, stop at the Chinese restaurant on Linden and Merrick." Precious had a craving for orange chicken, with beef and broccoli.

They arrived at the restaurant about an hour later. When Bryce got out of the car, he heard the faint sound of a tires screeching. Before he could turn around, someone yelled, "You should've paid the tab Johnson!" The statement was followed by the loud bark of gunfire. Bryce hit the deck, but when he heard the sound of his Maserati windshield shattering, his emotions went from panic to fear.

"Precious!" He jumped up and pulled her out of the car. Blood was everywhere. He wasn't sure if the blood was caused by the shattered glass, or if she was actually hit.

"Oh my god. Somebody call an ambulance," a lady who stepped out of the store yelled.

O rushed to the hospital as soon as he received the news. When he arrived at the ICU unit, Bryce was sitting on the bench in a zombie like state. He didn't seem to notice O and was oblivious to everything around him. The doctor walked up on O, stopping him before he could ask Bryce any questions.

The doctor had his hand on O's arm, as he shook his head from side to side. "Give him a minute. Right now, I doubt he's coherent enough to answer any questions you might have."

"What's the damage Doc? Is his wife gonna be alright?"

"Mrs. Johnson lost a lot of blood, but she's going to pull through." O sighed in relief, but then the doctor hit him with the second blow.

"We are trying to stabilize the fetus, but in the worse case scenario we are considering a C-section."

"Doc, do whatever it takes. Please!"

The doctor patted him on the shoulder. "Right now, you need to be there for your friend. I tried to offer him some words of comfort, but honestly, what do you tell a man after something like this?" The doctor left to tend to Precious, while O slowly approached Bryce.

For lack of anything better to say, he uttered, "Don't worry Bundy.

We'll find out who did this. Believe me, we're gonna make them pay!"

But when Bryce looked up at O, the look in his eyes gave O the chills. It was as if they showed no emotion. He simply stared through O as if he wasn't even there. What scared O the most was the fact that he recognized those eyes. The eyes staring at him didn't belong to Bryce Johnson; they belonged to Bundy.

Order Form

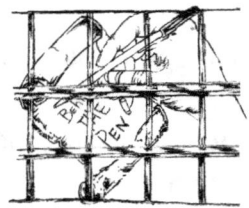

Behind The Pen Publishing, LLC
P.O. Box230239
Jamaica, NY 11423
www.BehindThePenPublishingLLC.com

Name: _____

Address: _____

City/State: _____

Zip: _____

QUANTITY	TITLE	PRICE	TOTAL
____	Stickin' & Movin'	$15.00	_____

Shipping/Handling (Via Priority Mail) $5.50 1-2 Books, $7.95 3-4 Books add $1.95 for ea. Additional book.

Total: $_____ FORMS OF ACCEPTED PAYMENTS: Institutional checks, money orders, US postal stamps. All mail in orders take 5-7 business days to be delivered.

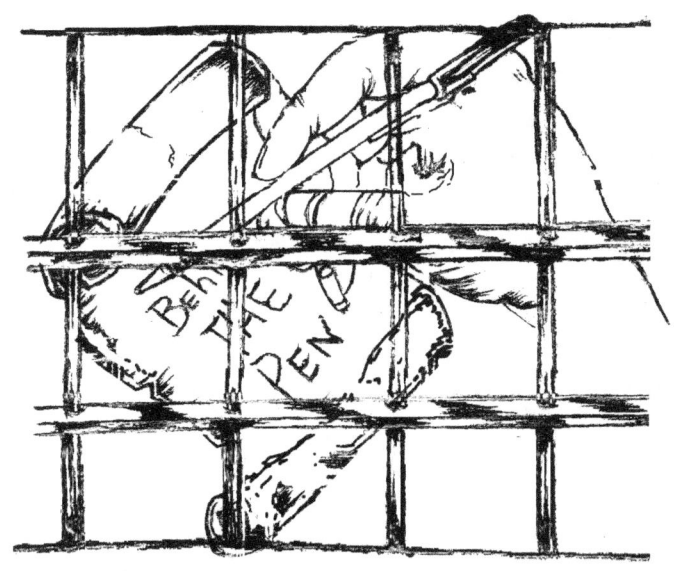

Behind The Pen Publishing, LLC would like to help writers achieve their dreams and become published authors.

B.T. P. is accepting Manuscripts. Please send the 1st 3 typed chapters to Behind The Pen Publishing.

Contact us at:

Behind The Pen Publishing, LLC
P.O. Box230239
Jamaica, NY 11423
BehindThePenPublishingLLC.com
www.facebook.com/ShawnBundyTaylor
or email: ShawnTaylor@BehindThePenPublishingLLC.com

NOTE: "These 3 chapters will not be returned."